"So—you don't want to see me again?"

Matthew's voice was harsh, and Rachel closed her eyes against the treacherous desire she had to reach out and touch him.

"I just think I'm rather—tired," she got out, opening her eyes again. For a heart-stopping moment she caught his brooding gaze. And it was electric. The look that passed between them owed nothing to the conversation they'd just had.

And then it was gone. Like a fire that was suddenly extinguished, his eyelids descended, and she was left with the uncanny suspicion that she'd imagined the whole thing.

Wishful thinking, she thought bitterly as the door closed behind him. But why? Why, after all these years, was she even considering that she might have made a mistake by walking out on him...?

ANNE MATHER began her career by writing the kind of book she likes to read—romance. Married, with two teenage children, this author has become a favorite with readers of romance fiction the world over—her books have been translated into many languages and are read in countless countries. Since her first novel was published in 1970, Anne Mather has written more than eighty romances, with over ninety million copies sold!

Books by Anne Mather

Don't miss any of our special offers. Write to us at the following address for information on our newest releases.

Harlequin Reader Service
901 Fuhrmann Blvd., P.O. Box 1397, Buffalo, NY 14240
Canadian address: P.O. Box 603,
Fort Erie, Ont. L2A 5X3

ANNE MATHER

a relative betrayal

Harlequin Books

TORONTO • NEW YORK • LONDON
AMSTERDAM • PARIS • SYDNEY • HAMBURG
STOCKHOLM • ATHENS • TOKYO • MILAN

Harlequin Presents first edition November 1990
ISBN 0-373-11315-3

Original hardcover edition published in 1990
by Mills & Boon Limited

Printed in U.S.A.

CHAPTER ONE

'RACHEL'S coming!'

'Is she?' Matthew had had plenty of opportunities during the long nights since Barbara's death to face that possibility—and decide he didn't give a damn.

'Yes.' His mother-in-law pressed the palms of her hands together. 'She'll be staying at the vicarage, of course.'

'Of course.'

Matthew was annoyingly indifferent, and Mrs Barnes shook her head. 'Well, someone had to invite her!' she exclaimed, as if needing to defend her position. 'Barbara was her cousin, after all.'

Matthew abandoned any attempt to answer any one of the dozens of letters that had flooded in since his wife had died, and got up from behind his desk. 'I'm not saying you shouldn't have done it, am I?' he asked wearily, pushing back the unruly weight of hair from his forehead. 'For God's sake, Maggie, you can invite who you like. It's your daughter's funeral, not some bloody garden party!'

'Oh, Matt!'

His harsh words achieved what he had been most hoping to avoid. His mother-in-law dissolved into noisy tears, and Matthew was obliged to take her in his arms and comfort her. But who was going to comfort him? he wondered bitterly, as the garrulous little woman's tears soaked through the grey silk of his shirt. God, he wished this whole charade was over! Perhaps then he'd find some meaning to his life; some peace.

Mrs Barnes at last composed herself sufficiently to draw back from him, patting the patch of wet cloth on his chest with a rueful hand. 'Oh, dear,' she said looking

5

up at him with misty eyes. 'You must forgive me. But I get so upset every time I think about it.'

'I know.' Matthew managed a polite smile, hoping against hope that she would leave now. It was strange, but since Barbara had died the house seemed to have been full of people, and he desperately wanted to be alone, however selfish that might be.

But, of course, his mother-in-law had something more to say. 'I didn't want to ask her, you know,' she confided, and he didn't need to be reminded who she was talking about. 'No. It was Geoffrey—he insisted. But then, she's *his* relation, isn't she? Not mine.'

Matthew heaved a sigh. 'It doesn't matter, Maggie.' He propped his lean hips against his desk and waited. Surely she would go now? He didn't know how much more of this he could take.

'Oh, well.' Mrs Barnes gave him a wistful look. 'So long as you understand I had nothing to do with it.' She paused, and then added anxiously, 'I hope there won't be any trouble. For Barbara's—and for Rosie's—sake.'

'I'm sure there won't be.'

Matthew could hear his voice losing all expression, and he was amazed that his mother-in-law could remain so totally unaware of it. But then, she had never been particularly perceptive, he reflected grimly. Or Barbara would never have succeeded in convincing her that their marriage had ever been anything more than a sham.

'Where is Rosie?' she asked now, and Matthew strove to contain his impatience.

'I don't know,' he replied tautly, glancing towards the long, mullioned windows. 'About the estate somewhere, I suppose. Perhaps she's down at the stables. I really have no idea.'

'You wouldn't like me to find her and take her home to the vicarage, would you?' Mrs Barnes suggested hopefully. 'I mean—I'm sure Agnes does a fine job but she's not like—family. Is she?'

Matthew pushed himself away from the desk. He could imagine his daughter's reaction if he told her she was going home with her grandmother, and it wasn't fit for his mother-in-law's consumption. 'I—think I'd rather she stayed here,' he declared, choosing his words with discretion. 'Agnetha's fairly competent, and Rosie has to get used to—to the situation.'

'I know, but——'

Mrs Barnes looked as if she was about to have a relapse, and, although Matthew despised himself for his lack of sympathy, he had to prevent another display of emotion. 'I think it'll be easier on you this way,' he declared, walking past her to the heavy door and opening it. 'And now I must beg your indulgence and get on. There's such a lot to do; you understand?'

'Of course, of course.' Mrs Barnes dabbed her eyes with the lace handkerchief she had taken from her pocket, and walked reluctantly towards him. 'But you will let me know if you need any help, won't you?' She paused beside him, looking up into his dark face through tear-drenched eyes. 'I know that's probably a silly thing to say. And I'm sure you feel you've all the help you need. But, at times like this, families should stick together.'

Matthew felt as if the smile he offered was merely a stretching of his facial muscles. But it evidently satisfied his mother-in-law, which had been his intention. 'Thanks,' he said, bending to bestow a dutiful kiss on her cheek. 'I'll be in touch.'

'Do.'

She wiped her eyes one more time, raised a hand in farewell and departed. Matthew waited to ensure that Watkins was there to see her out, and then went back into the library and closed the door.

Leaning back against it, he surveyed without emotion the pile of letters and cards awaiting his attention. So many people had written; so many business colleagues, or acquaintances, who had felt it their duty to offer their condolences. They had hardly known Barbara, but that didn't matter. The tragic circumstances of her demise had overruled formalities. There was a unifying quality about death that brought people who were virtual strangers together, and it was up to him to respond to their kindness.

But it was difficult, *bloody* difficult, he acknowledged grimly, straightening away from the door and making his way across the room. A tray of drinks resided on a table in the chimney alcove, and it was to this that he headed, pouring himself a stiff Scotch and drinking it straight down. Then, before replacing the stopper in the crystal decanter, he poured another and carried it over to his desk.

'My dear Matt,' he read tersely, 'We were so sorry to read of your tragic bereavement...' The words of the letter on the top of the pile leapt out at him, and he flung himself down on to his chair and closed his eyes. 'So sorry to read of your loss'—'our deepest sympathy in this time of mourning'—'so sorry to hear of Barbara's death'—the trite phrases were endless! He didn't even need to read them to know what each and every one of them would say. They all talked of Barbara's illness, her tragic death at the age of only thirty-two, of his loss. *His loss*...

His nerves tightened. How could you be married to someone for almost ten years, and yet still feel so little remorse at her passing? He and Barbara had been man and wife; they had produced a daughter, for God's sake! But there had never been any love between them—just a greed for money and possessions on her part, and a desire for revenge on his.

He opened his eyes again and, sitting up in his seat, he swallowed half the whisky in his glass. It was no good, he told himself tautly. He was getting maudlin, and for all the wrong reasons. Barbara was dead. Whatever she had done in life was over. He had to think of the future. Of Rosemary's future, at least. Maggie had been right about one thing. Agnetha was not family—and his daughter took advantage of that.

He groaned suddenly and ran weary fingers through the over-long hair at the nape of his neck. Rachel was

coming to the funeral! he thought savagely, acknowledging for the first time the real reason why he had been
so impatient with his mother-in-law. It had been all very
well telling himself he didn't care what she did when the
chances of her taking time off from her job in London
and making the long journey to Cumbria had seemed
so unlikely. But now, faced with the reality that
tomorrow he was going to see her again, his reactions
were not half as positive.

A tentative knock at the door put his thoughts to flight
and, glad of the interruption, Matthew lay back in his
chair. 'Come in,' he called, and Patrick Malloy, his secretary and personal assistant, put his head into the room.

'Sorry to intrude——' he began, and then, realising
Matthew was alone, he opened the door a little wider
and stepped inside. 'Oh—has Mrs Barnes gone?'

'As you see,' remarked his employer flatly, throwing
the remainder of the whisky to the back of his throat.
He held his glass out towards the other man. 'Get me
another, Pat, will you?'

Patrick closed the door behind him and crossed the
floor. 'It's a little early, even for you, isn't it?' he commented, with the familiarity of their long association,
but he took the glass and did as he was bidden. 'What
happened? Did she tell you she's inaugurating a Barbara
Conroy Memorial Fund?'

Matthew's head swung round. 'She's not, is she?' His
dismay was evident, and Patrick shook his head.

'Not that I know of,' he reassured him drily, handing
over a rather smaller measure of Scotch than Matthew
had previously poured for himself. He waited until his
employer had taken a generous mouthful. 'You look
shattered, do you know that?' He paused. 'So—what
did she want?'

Matthew expelled his breath heavily, and then lifted
guarded grey eyes to Patrick's face. 'Rachel's coming,'
he said simply, and the other man caught his breath.

'I see.'

'Do you?' Matthew got up from his chair again and paced across to the windows. 'Who'd have thought it, hmm? Rachel—coming to Barbara's funeral.' His lips twisted. 'Do you think she's coming to gloat?'

'You know Rachel's not like that,' retorted Patrick at once, but Matthew was unconvinced.

'Do I?' he countered, turning back to face his friend. 'I don't know anything about Rachel any more. It's been over ten years, Pat. Ten years!'

'I know.' Patrick's angular features were troubled. 'So, how do you feel about it?'

Matthew looked grim. 'The truth?'

'Of course.'

'Then—angry. Bloody angry!' said Matthew violently. 'I don't want her here. I wish to God I didn't even have to see her. It's been too long. Too many years. If it weren't for Rosemary, I'd probably never see any of the Barneses again after tomorrow.'

Patrick inclined his head towards Matthew's glass. 'Is that why you're drowning your sorrows in Scotch?' he enquired, not without some irony, and his employer scowled.

'I'm not drowning my sorrows,' he retorted curtly. 'I'm just trying to get through the next couple of days with some dignity.'

'And afterwards?'

Matthew frowned. 'What do you mean—afterwards?'

'I mean after the funeral. Have you thought what you're going to do about Rosemary? Now that—now that Barbara's not here any more, don't you think you ought to consider sending her away to school?'

Matthew sighed. 'Is that what you think?'

Patrick was ambivalent. 'She does need discipline,' he pointed out evenly. 'And unless you're going to spend more time at Rothmere——'

'Take up the life of a gentleman farmer, is that what you mean?' Matthew was sardonic.

'It's what your father would have wanted you to do,' replied Patrick quietly. 'And you know how your mother feels.'

'Yes.' Matthew acknowledged the fact that his mother would prefer him to live at home. But since his marriage to Barbara he had expended more and more energy attending personally to his business interests elsewhere, and spending most of his time away from the estate.

'Anyway,' Patrick could see his employer was becoming broodingly introspective, and quickly changed the subject, 'why don't you take Rosemary over to Helen's this afternoon? It would do you both good to get out of the house, and you know she and Gerald would be pleased to see you.'

Matthew considered the prospect of driving over to his sister's home near Ambleside, and shrugged. The idea of visiting the small hotel they ran overlooking Windermere was appealing, except that people might recognise him, and he wasn't in the mood to be sociable.

'I'll think about it,' he said without enthusiasm, finishing the whisky in a gulp. 'Do you know where Rosemary is, by the way? I haven't seen her since—well, since suppertime last night, actually.'

Patrick gave him a resigned look. 'So what's new?' he remarked, taking Matthew's empty glass from him and replacing it on the tray. 'Do you want me to find her? She'll be around somewhere.'

Matthew hesitated a moment, then he shook his head. 'No,' he said flatly, flexing his shoulders and walking towards the door. 'I'll catch her later.' He paused with his fingers on the handle. 'I'll be in the gym, if you want me. See you at lunch.'

He had skirted the hall and the drawing-room and was passing the morning-room when his mother called his name behind him. 'Matthew! Matthew, wait! Didn't Watkins tell you I was waiting to speak to you? Come into the parlour. I want to talk to you.'

Matthew's sigh was heartfelt, but, short of offending one of the few people he really cared about, he had little choice but to obey. 'I do have things to do, Mother,' he declared patiently, walking back towards her, and, remembering Watkins' face when he had shown Mrs Barnes out of the library, he guessed the old man had thought better of interrupting him.

'So do I,' responded Lady Olivia Conroy, pausing with her hand on the door, so that Matthew was forced to pass her on his way into the room. 'Ugh—you've been drinking! Matthew, it's barely twelve o'clock!'

'12.02, to be precise,' remarked Matthew evenly, halting in the centre of the softly fading Aubusson carpet. He thrust his hands into the pockets of the worn corded jacket he was wearing and faced her politely. 'What can I do for you?'

'You can stop adopting that supercilious attitude for a start,' said his mother shortly. 'Really, Matthew, I don't know what's the matter with you. I shouldn't have thought Barbara's death would have been such a shock; in the circumstances.'

Matthew regarded her dispassionately. 'What circumstances?'

'Oh, Matthew!' Clearly he was annoying her, but he didn't seem able to help it. 'You know what circumstances. The fact that Barbara had been ill for the better part of a year, and—and...'

'And?' he prompted.

'And you and she hadn't been close for—well, for years!'

Matthew inclined his head. 'I see.'

'What do you see?' Lady Olivia was obviously impatient. 'Matthew, please; I'm your mother. If there's something troubling you, then tell me. Ever since Barbara died I've tried to get close to you, but I can't. You're shutting me out. You're shutting everyone out! Darling, we're your family. Don't you think we deserve some consideration?'

'Oh, God!' Matthew's shoulders sagged. 'I'm not shutting anyone out, Mother. I just need some time alone, that's all. It's natural enough, isn't it?' He tried to be flippant. 'It's not every day one becomes a widower!'

His mother's expression was eloquent of her feelings. 'I think there's more to it than that,' she declared firmly. 'I'm not a fool, Matt. I know this marriage had its problems.'

'Its problems?' echoed Matthew caustically. 'Oh, yes.'

'So why are you acting as if you're grief-stricken?' countered his mother sharply. 'Helen tells me you haven't been over to see Gerald since you got back. Or the children. You know how Mark and Lucy dote on you. Goodness knows, you've always had more time for Helen's children than you have for your own daughter! What's the matter with you, Matt? Why are you behaving like this?'

Matthew turned away from her pained bewilderment, staring broodingly out of the long windows that overlooked the parterre at the side of the house. At this time of the year the lawns were edged with pansies and dwarf hyacinths, and the deep blue stems of salvias grew among clusters of cream and yellow saxifrage. Beyond the formal gardens, acres of rolling grassland swept away towards Rothmere Fell, and Matthew's eyes were drawn to the purple slopes where only sheep could scratch a living. When he was a boy, he had scrambled up those slopes with Brian Spencer, his father's shepherd, but nowadays he hardly gave them a thought. He left the running of the estate in his agent's hands, and spent his days attending board meetings and business lunches, and fighting a growing propensity for boredom.

'Matthew!'

His mother's voice arrested his wandering thoughts, and he forced himself to turn round again and face her. 'I'm listening.'

'You're not, or I'd have had some answers before now,' replied Lady Olivia tensely. 'What is it? Is it Rosemary? You know, something will have to be done about that child, before it's too late.'

Matthew regarded her frustrated face with some affection for a moment, and then flung himself on to one of the buttoned satin sofas that faced one another across a polished maplewood table. 'Did you know Rachel was coming to the funeral?' he enquired lightly, keeping his tone as casual as possible, and his mother gave a gasp.

'No!'

'Yes.' Matthew considered the toe of the boot he had propped disrespectfully on the corner of the table. 'Mrs Barnes gave me the news this morning. Apparently the Reverend invited her.'

Lady Olivia seemed to require some support herself now, for she sank down on to the sofa opposite her son and gazed at him disbelievingly. 'But why? Didn't he realise it was hardly in the best of taste?'

Matthew shrugged. 'As Maggie said, she is Barbara's cousin.'

'Is she in favour?' His mother was surprised.

'I wouldn't say that.' Matthew grimaced. 'But she's making the best of it. And it's true. Rachel is Barbara's cousin.'

'And your ex-wife!'

'So?'

'Matthew! Surely even you can see the unsuitability of your ex-wife attending your second wife's funeral?'

'Yes.' Matthew's stomach muscles clenched. 'But I can hardly stop her, can I? She is—family.'

'Family?' Lady Olivia's echo of the word was scathing. 'I don't know how you can suggest such a thing! I could say she was nothing but trouble from the moment you laid eyes on her. You were engaged to Cecily Bishop, do you remember? That's who you should have married.'

'I know.' Matthew's boot heel ground into the polished wood and his mother winced.

'Matt!'

'All right, all right.' Unable to sit still any longer, Matthew rose to his feet. 'And now, if you'll excuse me——'

'Is this why you've been so—so unapproachable?'

Matthew groaned. 'I haven't been unapproachable, Mother.'

'Yes, you have. You know you have.' Lady Olivia looked up at him despairingly. 'Oh, well—it will all be over tomorrow. Then you can get back to some semblance of normal living. I suggest you tell Mrs Barnes— and her husband—that you'll be incommunicado for a while. You don't want that awful woman coming here, treating this place as she did when Barbara was alive. If you make the position clear to begin with——'

Matthew's oath silenced her. 'Shut up, Mother, will you?' he muttered savagely, and, ignoring her shocked expression, he strode grimly out of the room.

In the gym, he changed into a pair of shorts and a vest, and stretched out on the lifting frame. The sheer physical effort it took to push the weights up the stack gave him some relief from the chaos of his thoughts, and the sweat he worked up helped to compensate for the alcohol he had consumed earlier. Then, when he was feeling pleasantly numb to anything but the physical aches and pains of his own body, he plunged into the jacuzzi and let the hot, pummelling jets revitalise his tortured muscles.

It was then that he admitted that he couldn't entirely dismiss what his mother had said. It was true that since Barbara had died he had felt a certain detachment from the events going on around him. His friends—those who had not been aware of the circumstances of his marriage, his acquaintances—probably thought it was grief; but his sorrow at the way things had turned out was a small thing by comparison. The truth was, Barbara's death had resurrected the past, and it wasn't until Mrs Barnes had told him Rachel was coming that he had realised exactly what he had been thinking.

And he despised himself for it! He couldn't still want her. Not after all this time. Not after all that had gone before. It was as he had told Patrick: he was angry, *bloody* angry, that she should have the nerve to come here.

So what if her uncle had invited her? So what if
Geoffrey Barnes had decided the occasion warranted her
presence? He was just a Church of England vicar. What
did he know?

She should have refused. She should have made some
excuse and stayed away, instead of embarrassing all of
them by joining in their grief. She wasn't sorry Barbara
was dead. What had Barbara been to her? Simply an
excuse for severing her marriage, so that she could pursue
the career that had always taken precedence in her life.

Matthew was drying himself when Patrick came to tell
him that lunch was on the table. 'And Rosemary's disappeared,' he announced, as Matthew stepped into worn
jeans and zipped them over his flat stomach. 'Do you
want me to go and look for her?'

'I'll do it myself—later,' replied his employer broodingly. 'And I'm not hungry. Make my excuses to my
mother, will you? I'll get a sandwich when I feel like it.'

CHAPTER TWO

THE place hadn't altered much architecturally over the years, Rachel decided. The road, which wound down from the Coniston Pass, still afforded a magnificent view of the valley, with Rothmere itself lying still and silent at its foot. From the pass, it was possible to see the roofs and chimneys of the house that stood at the end of the lake. Lower down, sturdy pines and spruce trees provided a protective screen from inquisitive eyes, except from the lake itself, where it was possible to catch a glimpse of the lawns and terrace at the front of the house. But, from the pass, Rachel looked down on the house that had once been her home, and knew a fleeting sense of nostalgia.

However, it didn't last. She had no wish to resurrect the past. She wouldn't be here at all were it not for Uncle Geoff, and she had no illusions that her aunt had endorsed the invitation. But Barbara had been her cousin, her uncle's only daughter, and if he wanted her here she owed him that, at least.

The village of Rothside, which was her destination, lay approximately halfway along the lake shore, with the waters of Rothdale Beck tumbling down from the fell and splitting the main street into two halves. Although there had been few structural changes, Rachel noticed how many of the cottages were now advertising accommodation available, and the old water-mill had been transformed into a café and gift shop. Evidently tourism had reached Rothside at last, and Rachel recognised her own profession's responsibility for that. It was due in part to the very successful job the media had done in promoting the Lake District that so many people now flocked to this most beautiful area of northern England.

And, while she regretted some of the changes that had
been made, the jobs the tourist industry had brought
had to have been welcome.

St Mary's church, and the vicarage that stood close
by, were situated on the outskirts of the village. But
Rachel was in no hurry to reach her destination. Instead, she parked her car outside the general stores—
which she noticed had been converted into a mini-
market—and went inside.

She hadn't expected to see anyone who knew her, but
the elderly woman in charge of the till was familiar. Mrs
Reed must have lived in Rothside for the past sixty years
at least, and she had always been regarded as a busybody.
However, not surprisingly after so long, she didn't immediately recognise Rachel in the slim, elegantly attired
young woman who stood just inside the door, and as
Rachel's clothes were evidently expensive she gazed at
her inquisitively.

'Can I help you?'

Rachel hid a smile and shook her head. 'I can manage,
thank you,' she said, picking up one of the wire baskets
and glancing along the shelves. It all looked very neat
and efficient, but she missed the familiar counter with
its tempting display of sweets and chocolate. Still, the
familiar things were there, if you looked for them:
locally produced honey, and Kendal mint cake. It was
only the way of exhibiting them that had changed. Much
like herself, she reflected cynically.

She carried her basket back to the check-out, and set
it on the low counter so that Mrs Reed could ring in on
the till the cost of the two items she had bought. Then,
as she retrieved her purse from her handbag, Mrs Reed
remarked, 'I don't suppose you got that tan in England?'

'No.' Rachel responded tolerantly. 'Um—the South
of France, actually,' she added, picking up her purchases. 'Thank you.'

But Mrs Reed was not about to let her go so easily.
Trade was obviously slack at this hour of a Monday

afternoon, and, leaving her seat, she accompanied Rachel to the door.

'I thought so,' she said. 'It's too early in the season for you to have caught any sun in this part of the country. You're not from around here, are you, dear?' Two beady brown eyes scanned Rachel's cool features. 'Yet, there's something about your face...'

Not wanting to have to identify herself now, Rachel reached for the handle of the door and pulled it open, just as it was propelled inwards from the other side. A girl of perhaps nine or ten years of age practically tumbled into the shop, regaining her balance with evident difficulty, and directing a hostile gaze at Rachel, as if she were totally to blame for what had happened.

'Oh—Rosemary!' exclaimed Mrs Reed, her expression registering a surprising amount of sympathy for the child. 'You haven't hurt yourself, have you, dear? You just opened the door at the wrong moment.'

'It was her fault!' retorted Rosemary, tossing back a single braid of night-dark hair, and fixing Rachel with an accusatory stare. 'Why don't you watch what you're doing? I could have broken my leg!'

Rachel caught her breath. 'Your neck would have been more appropriate,' she essayed smoothly, keeping her temper with an effort. 'Do you always stick it out so far?'

'Oh—there, don't take any notice of Rosemary's sulks!' exclaimed Mrs Reed quickly, evidently torn between the thought of losing an old customer and offending a new one. 'Rosemary's one of my best customers, aren't you, dear? Are you all right? No bones broken?'

But Rosemary was evidently not prepared to let anyone else speak for her. 'I should watch what I was saying, if I were you,' she informed Rachel, splaying her feet and placing balled fists on her jean-clad hips. 'My father's an important man in Rothside. One word from me, and you could find yourself in a load of trouble!'

Rachel gulped, strung between laughter and outrage. 'Are you threatening me?' she enquired, realising she was playing into the girl's hands by even taking her seriously, but unable to resist.

'Rosemary's not threatening anyone,' put in Mrs Reed, trying to make light of it. 'Are you, dear? And how is your dear daddy? You will tell him I was asking after him, won't you? We're all thinking about him, you know.'

Rosemary made no response to this, her small jaw jutting a little more aggressively as she met Rachel's amused gaze. Obviously, she was trying to think of something even more outrageous with which to shock her listeners, but the elderly shopkeeper forestalled her by asking what she wanted.

'Some sweeties?' Mrs Reed suggested, adopting a hopeful tone. 'Or how about a nice cold can of Coca Cola? I can get you one out of the fridge——'

'Just twenty kingsize, that's all,' the child interrupted her, pointing to the brand of cigarettes she wanted. 'Put them on Daddy's account. He'll settle with you later.'

'Now, Rosemary, you know I'm not supposed to sell cigarettes to a little girl of your age,' began Mrs Reed unhappily, and Rachel, seeing a chance to get away, decided to make good her escape. After the events of the last few minutes she had even less desire for Mrs Reed to recognise her, and she stepped outside, quelling the urge to retaliate.

But she hadn't even unlocked her car before the girl emerged from the store, opening the pack of cigarettes Mrs Reed had evidently not withheld, and putting one between her lips. If it was an act of defiance, it was one she had attempted many times before, thought Rachel irritably, trying to concentrate on juggling her purchases and her handbag, and getting the key in the lock. The way Rosemary extracted a book of matches from her pocket and applied a light to the cigarette proved it, and Rachel tried to tell herself it was nothing to do with her if the child's father sanctioned the offence.

'I hope you drive better than you walk!' Rosemary commented now, puffing on the cigarette, and, although she had at last got the car door open and was about to step inside, something inside Rachel snapped at the deliberate provocation.

Swinging round, she snatched the cigarette from the child's lips and the pack of cigarettes from her hand. Then, dropping them both on to the pavement, she ground her heel into them, watching Rosemary's face with an almost childlike sense of triumph as the pale, sallow features erupted into fury.

'How—how dare you?' she screamed, launching herself at Rachel with flailing arms and legs that somehow connected despite her diminutive size. 'You wait until I tell my father about you! You'll wish you'd never been born!'

'Let's both tell him, shall we?' taunted Rachel, losing all sense of reason with the situation. Twisting the child's hands behind her back, she turned her round so that Rosemary was unable to go on kicking her, adding, 'Where do you live? You might as well tell me. I'd like to meet this father of yours. I'd like to tell him what a disgusting little brat he's got for a daughter!'

'Let go of me!'

Rosemary continued to struggle, but it was obvious she was losing the battle, and there was a suspicious break in her voice that hinted of emotions hitherto not in evidence.

'Tell me where you live,' Rachel insisted, not making the mistake of losing her grip, and then sighed with some frustration when Mrs Reed came charging out of the shop.

'For heaven's sake!' she exclaimed, taking in the scene with horrified eyes. 'What is going on here? Rosemary, my dear! Is this lady bothering you?'

'You have to be joking!'

With a word that was not at all ladylike, and which Mrs Reed evidently recognised, judging from her expression, Rachel let the girl go and turned to the other woman. And Rosemary, who had evidently just been waiting for such an opportunity, took immediate advantage of the situation. While Rachel was forced to make some explanation of her actions, Rosemary aimed a booted foot at the wing of Rachel's car before scooting off across the footbridge over the stream.

Rachel was almost speechless. 'That—that child,' she choked, struggling to control her voice, 'that child is totally undisciplined!' She bent to examine a ladder in her dark tights and the purpling bruise below it. 'For heaven's sake, why did you serve her? I assume you knew the cigarettes were for her.'

'Of course I didn't.' Mrs Reed was not prepared to admit to that. 'Do you think I want to lose my licence? No—I thought they were for her father. And now, if you'll excuse me, I have work to attend to.'

'But who is she?' demanded Rachel testily, only to find she was talking to herself. Mrs Reed had apparently decided she had said too much already, and, with a feeling of frustration, Rachel flung open the door of the car.

It was then that she saw the dent in the panelling. Until that moment, Rosemary's fit of retaliation for the destruction of her cigarettes had scarcely registered. But now she saw what the child had done, and an anger she had scarcely known she possessed gripped her. The selfish little brat! she thought infuriatedly. If she could get her hands on her . . .

Coming to an impulsive decision, she closed and locked the car door again, and, grimacing at the heels of her handmade Italian shoes, she started off across the footbridge. She knew the village like the back of her hand, and unless Rosemary had disappeared into one of the cottages facing the beck she might just have a chance of catching her. The girl would not expect her to follow her, and might be dawdling. Rachel could only hope that luck was on her side now.

She attracted the attention of several pairs of eyes as she crossed the road at the other side of the stream and started up the steep lane that led away from the beck. Tourists in this area invariably wore comfortable walking shoes or boots, and dressed for the most part in hiking clothes and wind-cheaters. Rachel's long-jacketed suit of navy and white houndstooth and the fine white muslin blouse she wore beneath it were definitely not casual, and her air of purposeful assurance drew a curious speculation.

She wondered if anyone had recognised her yet, or whether her new hairstyle and town clothes were blinding people to her identity. Surely she hadn't changed that much? And with the funeral tomorrow they ought to make the association.

She abruptly abandoned these thoughts at the sight of a child loitering ahead of her. Although she was some distance away, the dark plait of hair was unmistakable. It was Rosemary; it had to be. And, as Rachel had supposed, she was totally unaware that she might have been followed.

Rachel took a deep breath and quickened her pace. There was no place to hide, and if Rosemary should happen to glance back and see her her chance might well be lost. And now that she was almost within reach of her goal she was curiously loath to prolong the agony. There was something unwillingly vulnerable about the girl's bent head and drooping shoulders. Without the memory of that scene outside the village stores, Rachel might almost have felt sorry for her. Who was she? Where was she going? And, more expediently, where did she live?

The lane, which was backed by the walled gardens of cottages that faced the fell, gave on to open countryside just a few yards further on. It was a narrow winding track that climbed between dry stone walls and rocky crags to the summit of Rothdale Pike. It was mostly used by sheep, or less adventurous climbers who wanted to reach the peak by a less arduous method than striking up the rock-face. Whatever, it was not really the kind of route for a girl of Rosemary's age to go wandering

up alone, and Rachel searched her mind, trying to remember if there were any farms within walking distance.

And then Rosemary glanced back and saw her.

Rachel didn't know what had drawn the child's attention. Maybe her heels had clattered on one of the
loose stones that covered the track. Although it had been
resurfaced at some time, snow and frost had left deep
delves in the paving, and there were plenty of pebbles
lying about. In any event, the girl had now recognised
her and, although her expression revealed her indignation, she was evidently not prepared to stay and fight
another losing battle.

Scrambling over the crumbling wall beside her, the
child struck off across the sloping hillside, her rubber-
soled shoes moving swiftly over the uneven surface.
Although Rosemary's legs were shorter than her pursuer's, Rachel guessed she hadn't a snowball in hell's
chance of catching her in her high heels, and she clenched
her fists frustratedly when the child turned and raised
her fingers in an insolent salute.

But even as Rachel stood, impotent beside the dry
stone barrier, a movement beyond Rosemary's taunting
figure drew her attention. A rider had appeared from
the trees that marked the lower slopes and was coming
swiftly towards them. The man—for she could see that
the rider was too big to be a woman—was mounted on
a great black horse, and even from this distance it was
possible to observe his expert horsemanship. It was years
since Rachel had been on a horse, and even then she
had never achieved the skill and sense of balance she
was presently admiring. The man and his mount moved
as a single entity, and Rachel's appreciation was such
that she briefly forgot her objective.

Rosemary, however, seemed unaware of anyone but
her pursuer, and it was only when the horseman seemed
in danger of riding the child down that Rachel realised
her vulnerability. Objectionable she might be, but Rachel
had no desire to see her get hurt, and, resting her hands
on the wall, she yelled, 'Look out, behind you!'

Rosemary's expression turned from scorn to disbelief to shocked awareness, all in swift succession, but before she could move or get out of the way the rider was upon her. He didn't ride her down though. On the contrary, with a skilled shortening of the reins he brought the powerful animal to a halt beside her, and as Rachel watched, open-mouthed, he swung the child up in front of him.

For a moment, Rachel was too shocked to do anything. She wasn't even sure what she was witnessing, or indeed if the scene that was being enacted before her eyes was really happening. It was a bright day, and concentrating on Rosemary's diminutive form in the face of a lowering sun had caused spots to dance before her eyes.

She blinked several times, and as she did so the horseman swung his mount around to head back the way he had come. There had been no cry of protest from the girl, and Rachel could only assume that she knew her rescuer. But that didn't absolve her of the damage she had done to Rachel's car, and, cursing her narrow skirt, Rachel clambered over the wall.

'Wait!'

Her cry hardly carried across the open moorland, competing as it did with thrushes and curlews, and the distinctive call of a blackbird. But her actions must have caught the man's attention, for he turned his head to look at her and she saw his face for the first time.

Dear God, it was *Matt*! she realised disbelievingly, the knowledge hitting her with a force she had never expected. For a moment it was as if the last ten years had rolled away, and her heart was pounding as it used to do every time she saw him. Nothing in her experience had prepared her for the shock of seeing him again, and although she fought to hold on to her composure she was suddenly trembling with the violence of her emotions.

But with this awareness came another shattering conclusion. The child—Rosemary—must be *his* daughter.

Her stomach clenched and her mouth dried. His daughter! The daughter he and Barbara had had soon after his divorce from Rachel herself.

But it was sobering, too, and as the proud stallion and his equally proud riders picked their way towards her she managed to salvage a little dignity. But never in her wildest dreams had she expected to meet Matt in circumstances like these, and she prayed she had the strength to hide how shaken it had left her.

She had no idea when Matthew had realised who she was. But as the enormous horse came nearer his guarded expression revealed that he had definitely identified her now. Not that that was any consolation. It was perfectly obvious that he was not pleased at meeting her like this. The grey eyes that she remembered so well were glacially distant, and the hands wrapped around the reins were taut within his wrist-length leather gloves.

Rosemary, meanwhile, was looking as if she was torn between the urge to confess her side of the story before Rachel had a chance to speak, and the equally strong suspicion that by saying nothing she could deny everything. You could almost see her weighing the pros and cons of confession, Rachel thought bitterly. No wonder Mrs Reed had refrained from making any derogatory remarks about the girl. The Conroys owned the vast proportion of the land hereabouts, and, like many of the cottages in Rothside, the lease on the store was owned by them.

The horse and his riders had reached her now, and Rachel thought how typical it was that she should be put at such a disadvantage. Her height had never put her on eye-level terms with Matthew, but on foot she had never had to look up at him this way. As it was, the ignominy of her position was not lost on his daughter, and Rosemary's lips curled maliciously as her trailing shoe drew temptingly close to Rachel's chin.

Deciding the best method of defending her position was by ignoring it, Rachel looked up at him with what she hoped was a cool, unflustered gaze. 'Hello, Matt,' she said evenly, briefly enjoying Rosemary's startled deflation. Evidently it had never occurred to her that Rachel might know her father.

She was not a pretty child, thought Rachel dispassionately, fleetingly aware of the similarities between her and her father. They were both dark, of course—dark-haired, and dark-skinned—but whereas Matthew's features were strong, and still disturbingly attractive, Rosemary's face was thin and decidedly sulky.

All the same, it was difficult to make any real assessment of the child with Matthew looking down at her. A different Matthew, yet still so familiar, despite the flecks of grey in his hair and the broader contours of his body. The Matthew she remembered had looked approachable, good-natured—not remote and brooding like this man. The Matthew she had fallen in love with would never have regarded her with quite that look of detachment, through eyes that, even narrowed, conveyed his raw dislike.

But Rosemary could not see her father's withdrawn expression, and his polite, 'Rachel,' in answer to her greeting was a cause for consternation.

'Daddy, I didn't do it!' she exclaimed, without waiting any longer for Rachel to incriminate her. 'It wasn't me! It was someone else! Oh, tell her I couldn't do a thing like that——'

Matthew drew his gaze from Rachel's face to look down at his daughter. 'What?' he demanded blankly. 'What are you talking about?' His eyes shifted unwillingly back to the young woman beside him. 'Do you know something about this?'

Rachel took a deep breath. 'Yes,' she admitted, half unwillingly now, and with a grim exclamation Matthew swung himself down from the saddle.

The horse shifted uncertainly at the sudden shift of weight from his back, but Matthew's hand on his muzzle swiftly reassured him. 'Rosemary?' he said, with an unmistakable inflection in his voice. 'Perhaps you'd explain. I'm waiting to hear what this is all about.'

Rachel expelled her breath warily. The annoyance of Rosemary's attack on her car was fast losing significance. Indeed, the more she thought about it, the more ridiculous it seemed for her to have come charging after the girl, when she was so unsuitably attired for such an expedition. As it was, her heels were scuffed, her tights were laddered, and whatever conviction she had started out with was rapidly diminishing.

'It wasn't my fault——' began Rosemary again, defensively, and, realising this was getting more complicated by the minute, Rachel intervened.

'We had—a—a misunderstanding,' she said, meeting the girl's sullen stare with determined coolness. Then, sensing that Matthew was looking at her again, she transferred her gaze to the open neck of his dark blue sweatshirt. 'It was something and nothing.' She shrugged. 'I didn't know who she was.'

'Would that have made a difference?'

His voice was clipped and without expression, and Rachel knew a rekindling sense of resentment. They were both the same, she thought. Father and daughter alike. They were both treating her with the kind of arrogant contempt more suitably reserved for an inferior, and, although moderation warred with defiance, she refused to let either of them walk all over her.

'No,' she replied now, turning to make her rocky retreat over the pile of stones. She refused to stand there and argue with him like some recalcitrant minion. She would pay for the repairs to her car, and to hell with him. She had no intention of begging compensation from the Conroys.

But, as she struggled to climb back into the lane, and her feet slid ignominiously over the rocks, Rosemary giggled. It was a boastful little sound that jarred Rachel's senses, and she was unbearably tempted to turn back and take up the attack. Her fingers itched to wipe the triumphant smile from the girl's face, but she resisted the impulse. Discretion is the better part of valour, she repeated to herself, like a mantra, and concentrated on getting over the wall and safely on to solid ground.

'Rachel!'

Matthew's harsh use of her name was briefly compelling, scraping over her nerves like a rough hand on soft skin. How many times had she heard him use that word in just that way when he had been making love to her? she wondered unwillingly. How many times had he been compelled to abandon whatever plans he had to haul her back into his arms and lose himself in her willing body? Her hands clenched. Just as he had lost himself in Barbara's body, she appended bitterly. She mustn't forget that.

By the time she had slithered down into the ditch at the other side of the wall, Matthew was waiting for her. His booted feet had made short shrift of the crumbling rocks, and he offered her his hand to breach the gap between the ditch and the road. Pretending she hadn't seen it, Rachel made her own progress up on to the road, and then stopped to make another examination of her appearance. Damn! she swore. There were at least half a dozen runs in her stockings now, and her hands were scraped and sore. So much for revenge, she thought frustratedly. All she had succeeded in doing was making a complete fool of herself.

'*Rachel!*'

Matthew's hand on her arm would have swung her round to face him, but she shrugged it off and started back down the lane. To hell with the Conroys—*all* the Conroys, she thought childishly. She should never have agreed to come here. It had definitely been a mistake.

'Rachel, for heaven's sake!' Matthew's tone was distinctly angry now and, after ordering Rosemary to get down from the horse, he came striding after her. 'You might as well tell me. You didn't come after her just for the fun of it.'

Rachel halted reluctantly. 'It's not important,' she declared coldly, angry herself that her quickening breath wasn't just a result of her exertions. 'I've got to go. Uncle Geoff will be wondering where I am.'

'To hell with Uncle Geoff!' retorted Matthew unfeelingly, glancing back over his shoulder to assure himself that Rosemary had indeed done as he had said. Then, transferring his gaze back to Rachel, he arched dark brows. 'Well?'

'I'm not a child, Matt.' Rachel resented his high-handed demand that he should be put in the picture. 'As I said, it's not important. Now—if you'll excuse me——'

'Rachel!'

Instinctively he reached out and grasped her wrist, his action born of his frustration, but Rachel was furious. Lifting her eyes to his, she forced herself to stare him down and, after a pregnant moment, he released her.

'Goodbye, Matt,' she said distantly, and, refusing to prolong a situation that she was no longer certain she could control, she stalked stiffly away.

CHAPTER THREE

'I'll see you back at the vicarage.'

Rachel stood beside the long black saloon that was waiting to take her aunt and uncle back to Rothmere House, cool and remote in her black suede skirt and matching jacket. The sombre colour of her outfit drew attention to the silvery lightness of her hair, and, although she kept it shorter these days, and swept back behind her ears, its paleness accentuated the unnatural pallor of her cheeks.

She knew she looked pale. She could feel it. The service in the village church had been more of a strain than she could have realised, and the awareness of Matthew and his mother in the pew in front of her had added to her discomfort. What had he been thinking? she wondered. What feelings of grief and remorse had filled his thoughts to the exclusion of all else? Sadness, of course, and pity; but was he as heartbroken as Aunt Maggie had maintained? Somehow she doubted it. The man she had met out on the fells had not looked heartbroken. Bitter, perhaps, and angry. But not torn by any overwhelming pangs of emotional anguish. And why should *she* expect anything else, after what he had done to her?

The Bishop of Norbury had conducted the service, leaving Uncle Geoff to mourn the loss of his daughter in private. And afterwards Barbara's remains had been buried in the family plot in the adjoining graveyard. The bishop himself had read the eulogy, before the heavy, iron-bound casket had been lowered into the ground, and the sound of Aunt Maggie's weeping had echoed off the surrounding headstones.

But now the ceremony was over, and a long stream of limousines was already transporting family and friends back to the house, where a cold buffet was waiting. Personal respects would be endorsed, sympathy would be offered, and then everyone would depart about their own business, guiltily relieved that their responsibility was over.

'What do you mean?' Rachel's aunt demanded now, putting aside her grief to lean out of the car window and gaze up at her niece with an aggravated impatience. 'You'll see us back at the vicarage? What is that supposed to mean?'

'Please, Maggie!' Geoffrey Barnes put a detaining hand on his wife's arm, but she shook him off.

'Stop it, Geoff!' she exclaimed irritably. 'Well, Rachel? I'm waiting for an answer.'

Rachel glanced about her; unwillingly aware that their exchange was attracting curious eyes. Not least because their car was holding up at least half a dozen other limousines.

'I think it would be better if I went straight back to the vicarage, Aunt Maggie,' she responded quickly. 'I— well, it's not as if I'd be a welcome visitor at the house, and I'm sure I'd save us all a deal of embarrassment if I left you and Uncle Geoff to accept everyone's condolences alone.'

Her aunt's face suffused with colour. 'You should have thought of that before you came here,' she hissed angrily, her grief apparently taking second place to her indignation. 'But you had to come, didn't you? You had to have your—your pound of flesh!'

'Aunt Maggie!'

Rachel was horrified that her aunt should believe she had come here with some perverted desire to bear witness to her cousin's demise. Whatever Barbara had done, she had not deserved to die, and Rachel felt only pity now for the woman who had destroyed her marriage.

'Maggie, for goodness' sake!'

Geoffrey Barnes's face mirrored his distaste at this unpleasant scene, and Rachel felt the unaccustomed sting of tears behind her eyes. Dear God, and she had felt obliged to come here because she had thought—foolishly, she now realised—that they needed her.

'I don't care.' Her aunt was unrepentant. 'She's here now, and I will not have people saying that she wasn't invited to the house. How do you think that would look? People talk, Geoffrey. Before you know it, they'd be saying that Matt didn't invite her because he's afraid to see her——'

'Oh, Aunt Maggie!' Rachel was almost speechless with emotion. 'That—that is absolutely—ridiculous!'

'I know it and you know it, but *they* don't,' retorted her aunt grimly. 'Now, will you get in the car and stop behaving as if your presence at Rothmere had any importance—any importance at all?'

Rachel hesitated, but to argue any further would only aggravate an already embarrassing situation, and when her aunt thrust open the door she unwillingly stepped inside. But, once installed on one of the folding seats facing her aunt and uncle on the leather banquette opposite, she spoke to her uncle.

'What do you think, Uncle Geoff?' she asked him tensely. 'Don't you feel it would be better if I didn't accompany you?'

'Geoff——' began her aunt warningly, but for once Geoffrey Barnes didn't need his wife's admonishments.

'I suspect Maggie may be right,' he ventured, to Rachel's dismay, running a nervous finger around the inside of his clerical collar. 'Rothside isn't like London, Rachel. And people do gossip, I regret to say. Your coming here is bound to have caused conjecture, and avoiding speaking to Matthew will only fuel the fires of speculation.'

Rachel caught her breath. 'Then why did you invite me?'

'You might well ask,' declared her aunt darkly, dabbing at her eyes with a lace handkerchief.

'I invited you because Barbara is—was—your cousin, and I saw this as a way to resolve our differences,' declared Geoffrey Barnes firmly. 'Rachel, when your father thrust the responsibility of your upbringing upon us all those years ago, I did not see it only as a physical duty. You are our niece, whatever else. Can't we forgive the past?'

Rachel moistened her lips and looked out of the window of the car. Forgive the past? she echoed silently. How was that possible? Obviously Aunt Maggie forgave nothing, and, for herself, she wanted no part of any attempt at reconciliation with the Conroys.

'You do see how it would look, don't you, Rachel?' her uncle persisted now, and Rachel managed a slight inclination of her head in his direction. But inside she was a churning mass of nervous tension that not even her media training could totally control.

The procession of cars was sweeping through the stone gates that marked the southern boundary of Rothmere House now, and Rachel's fingers clenched around her handbag as the remembered lawns and paddocks opened out beside her. Rothside had been recognisable to her, but the grounds of Rothmere were unbearably familiar. Yet, if it hadn't changed in over two hundred years, why should she have expected it to change in only ten? Didn't it only go to prove that no one was indispensable? The passing of Rachel Barnes Conroy hadn't even ruffled the surface of the lake that lapped the pebbled shore below the house.

The house itself was solidly built of lakeland stone, with long mullioned windows glinting in the late afternoon sunlight. It was built on three floors, with many turrets and chimneys, and Rachel had always thought it had many of the characteristics of one of the fortified manor houses of earlier times, but Matthew had declared it was because it had been added to so many times that it had lost its own identification. But, in spite of everything, Rachel had loved the house, and seeing it again now was a particularly painful experience.

Watkins was waiting on the gravelled forecourt, to open car doors and welcome his employer's guests to

Rothmere, and his old eyes widened in some amazement when Rachel stepped first from the limousine.

'Why—it's Miss Rachel!' he exclaimed. And then, recollecting the circumstances, his lined features sobered. 'Um—good afternoon, Mrs—*Miss* Barnes.'

'Rachel will do,' she responded gently, acknowledging his look of gratitude as she turned away to draw a deep breath. Well, here she was, she thought tensely. Let battle commence!

Her aunt and uncle were climbing out of the limousine now, and, meeting Aunt Maggie's accusing gaze, Rachel guessed she had witnessed the exchange between herself and Watkins. But what of it? she asked herself defensively. She had always had a soft spot for the elderly butler, and of all the servants at Rothmere he had been the first to accept her as Matthew's wife. If only Watkins were the only one to meet.

In the event, she was able to join the subdued group of people thronging the hall of Rothmere House without incident. Remaining behind her aunt and uncle, she attracted little immediate attention, and only when they made their way across the room to speak to Matthew and his mother did she feel the urge to hang back. But Aunt Maggie was having none of that, and, grasping her by the arm, she forced her to accompany them.

'You must remember the good times, Matt,' someone was saying as they approached, and with a pang Rachel wondered how popular Barbara had been.

'Matt, we're here,' Maggie was saying now, interrupting the speaker to tug arrogantly at Matthew's arm, and Rachel wished the floor would open up and swallow her. She didn't want to be here. She didn't want to be a part of this very personal occasion. And, most of all, she didn't want to speak to the man who had once been the whole core of her existence.

He was looking exceptionally composed for a bereaved man, she thought bitterly. Tall, and dark, and attractive, his sombre attire only adding to his air of controlled sophistication. He didn't look like a man who had just lost his much-loved wife, but then Matt had always had the uncanny ability to hide his feelings, she remembered.

'Maggie, Geoff,' he responded now, allowing his mother-in-law to bestow a fervent kiss on his cheek before his eyes moved beyond her to the young woman who hung back from their intimate circle. 'Rachel,' he added stiffly, and she had, perforce, to step forward and offer her own condolences.

'I'm sorry,' she said, aware that his use of her name had attracted more than one pair of eyes. 'Please—believe me.'

'Oh, I do.'

But Matthew's eyes were cold, his expression as hard and unforgiving as that of the slim, elderly woman standing at his side. Lady Olivia had reacted violently to his use of Rachel's name, but like her son she would not make a scene in public.

'Rachel,' she echoed, but her lips were thin and forbidding. It was obvious how she felt, and Rachel shivered in spite of the press of bodies around her.

'Lady Olivia,' she responded, steeling herself against the almost uncontrollable urge to escape. 'This is a very sad occasion.'

Matthew's mother's lips twisted. 'Yes,' she said. 'It is.' But the meaning behind her words was obscure, and Rachel was glad when someone else came to claim Lady Olivia's attention.

Several white-coated attendants, hired for the occasion, were making their way among the guests with trays of glasses containing sherry or whisky, and the huge doors to the dining-room had been opened up to display the sumptuous cold buffet laid out on damask-covered tables. As people relaxed, and cigars were lit, a haze of tobacco smoke rose above the gathering, and the level of sound gradually rose in volume.

Rachel, compelled to accept at least one drink before making her escape, allowed herself to be engulfed in the mêlée. Her aunt and uncle were paying little attention to her now, her aunt, at least, enjoying the dubious notoriety of being the mother of the deceased. Her uncle seemed less aware of his surroundings, and she guessed that for him this was something of an ordeal. But at least he had his faith to sustain him, she thought ruefully. For herself, she had no such panacea.

It was time to leave, she decided grimly. She had done what Aunt Maggie had demanded she do and paid her respects, but now it was time for her to go. Perhaps, in spite of Uncle Geoff's invitation, she should have stayed away. It was obvious that Matthew's mother thought so. And Matt, too, although he was probably enjoying her discomfort. Whatever, she couldn't wait to put as many miles as possible between herself and this painful exhumation of the past.

Putting down her glass, she began to thread her way back across the hall. Occasionally someone recognised her, and rather stilted greetings were exchanged, but on the whole she avoided any further embarrassment. Happily, they were all too busy helping themselves to the mouth-watering canapés that were presently being circulated, and swallowing more of Matt's extremely good Scotch. It had turned into just another cocktail party, thought Rachel, somewhat cynically, depression settling like a heavy weight upon her shoulders.

She was within a few yards of the door when the accident happened. Someone stepped back heavily on to her toe, and she had to choke back the automatic protest that sprang to her lips. But even as she struggled to restrain her indignation the perpetrator of her injury pushed rudely past her, and she realised belatedly exactly who it was.

'Wait a minute!' she exclaimed, forgetting for a moment where she was as she lunged forward awkwardly and grasped the child's arm. Balancing on her uninjured foot, she swung the girl round to face her, only to wish she hadn't when she saw Rosemary's tear-stained face.

'What do you want?' the little girl asked defensively, evidently recognising her, and Rachel wondered what particular malevolent god had chosen that she should make one abysmal mistake after another.

'Um—nothing,' she said abruptly, releasing her and lifting the offended foot from her shoe to rub it tenderly against the calf of her other leg. 'Forget it.'

Rosemary hesitated. 'I suppose you're expecting me to thank you for not telling my father what happened yesterday,' she declared suddenly, and Rachel looked up from examining the purpling bruise on her instep to find the child still confronting her.

'I beg your pardon?'

'Is that why you're here?' Rosemary demanded suspiciously. 'I heard Grandma tell Daddy that you wouldn't dare to come here to the house, but you're here now, so is that why?'

Rachel slid her foot back into her shoe and expelled a careful breath. 'Your—your mother was my cousin,' she said, after an awkward moment. 'That's why I'm here. Not—not for any other reason.'

Rosemary frowned. 'Then why haven't I seen you before? If you're really Mummy's cousin, why haven't you come to visit?'

Rachel hesitated now. 'It's a long story——'

'And not one for your ears, rabbit,' remarked a cool, crisp voice behind them. 'What's going on here? Aren't you supposed to be helping Mrs Moffat in the kitchen?'

Rachel stiffened. The dark, velvety tones of her ex-husband's voice were unmistakable, and she didn't need to see Rosemary's instinctive reaction to his words to know who had joined them.

'I don't want to help Mrs Moffat,' Rosemary mumbled now, casting an appealing look in her father's direction. 'You only want me to stay out of the way. You don't really care what I want to do!'

Matthew moved into Rachel's line of vision, and, although she was loath to study his dark features, his daughter's words were so startling that she felt compelled to observe his expression.

'I think you've done quite enough, Rosemary,' he declared, his tone still even, but icily remote. 'And as you prefer to be defiant rather than enjoy yourself in the kitchen, I suggest you find Agnetha and have her put you to bed. You'll really be out of the way then, won't you?'

'No!'

Rosemary's cry was anguished, a mixture of indignation and desperation, a frantic appeal to his finer feelings, but Matthew was not to be persuaded.

'Bed, Rosemary,' he said implacably, gesturing towards the inner hallway and the staircase which, Rachel knew from experience, curved elegantly around its panelled walls.

Rachel wanted to protest. She found herself wanting to say that perhaps Matthew's judgement had been a little harsh, and that Rosemary's remarks might have a grain of truth in them. But she didn't. She didn't know enough about the situation to warrant making some unguarded comment, and besides, her own experiences with Rosemary were hardly grounds for encouragement. It was nothing to do with her, she told herself firmly. Just because, for a moment there, she had felt a reluctant pang of sympathy for the child, there was no reason to get involved in what was possibly a long-running battle between them.

There was a pause then, when Rachel half expected the girl to exhibit some further show of defiance, but it passed. With artificially bright eyes and only the faintest reddening of her nose to betray her emotions, Rosemary marched away towards the stairs, and Rachel was left to confront the child's father with her defensive shell not quite intact.

Around them, the silence which had descended when Rosemary had challenged her father was quickly replaced. Although Rachel was sure that Matthew's other guests would all have liked to go on listening to their exchange, politeness, and embarrassment that they might be observed, forced them to contrive an air of normality.

'Matt,' she murmured stiffly now, using his name as both an acknowledgement and a farewell, then, walking rather gingerly on her still-painful instep, she started again towards the door.

'Rachel!'

Matthew's impatient summons was all too familiar, but she pretended not to hear. If she could just make it out on to the forecourt, she was sure she could persuade one of the liveried chauffeurs from the funeral directors to take her back to the vicarage, and once there she intended to pack and leave before her aunt and uncle noticed she was missing. Cowardly perhaps, but justifiable under the circumstances.

'Rachel!'

This time, Matthew's hand gripping the yielding flesh of her upper arm was determined. It was not like that other occasion, when there had been only the sheep and the birds that inhabited Rothdale Pike to observe them. Here, not only were they the cynosure of those eyes near enough to see what was happening, but their words could be overheard by as many people as cared to listen.

Clenching her teeth, she looked up at him, willing him as she had done before to let her go, but this time he chose not to obey her silent command. 'I think we should talk, Rachel,' he said, his voice just as cool and deadly as it had been when he'd spoken to his daughter. 'Now— or later. It's all the same to me.'

Rachel took a steadying breath. 'Why?' she countered tensely, refusing to let him intimidate her, and his eyes narrowed.

'Why do you think?' he retorted. 'I want you to tell me why you followed Rosemary from the village yesterday. You were following her, weren't you? In spite of what she says.'

'What does she say?' asked Rachel unwillingly, curious to know how the child had defended herself, but Matthew was having none of that.

'I want to hear your story,' he told her, without releasing her arm, and Rachel's face flamed. He was treating her like a child, too, she thought indignantly. And embarrassing her as well, today of all days.

'I should have thought you had more important things to think about,' she countered hotly, keeping her voice low with an effort. 'Matt, please—are you trying to humiliate me? Wasn't what happened ten years ago enough for you?'

Matthew's grey eyes narrowed. 'Humiliating *you*?' he echoed, barely audibly, and this time she had no fear that anyone else could overhear his harsh denial. 'Humiliating you? Oh, Rachel, you don't know the meaning of the word!'

'Matt! Matt, I've been looking everywhere for you!' As Matthew's hand fell away from Rachel's arm, Lady Olivia insinuated herself between them, her eyes, so like her son's, assessing in an instant the potential danger in the situation. Lady Olivia hadn't been looking for Matt, decided Rachel bitterly—although her interruption had probably not come a moment too soon. She had known exactly where he was all the time, and she had undoubtedly made a beeline for them. 'There are people waiting to speak to you,' she added, sliding her arm through his and circumventing any further exchange between the protagonists. 'Rachel,' she murmured, in much the same way as Rachel had used Matthew's name earlier, and, refusing to be diverted, she drew her son away.

With no further obstacle to her departure now, Rachel felt suddenly loath to go. Even though she was aware that the little scene that had just concluded had not totally removed the covert glances being cast in her direction, she no longer felt the need to escape. The worst had happened. Matt had revealed his hatred for her, and embarrassed her in front of his friends. What more could he do to her?

CHAPTER FOUR

In the event, Rachel had to send for a taxi to take her back to the vicarage. And, in consequence, she was still gathering her things together when she heard the crunching sound of a limousine's wheels on the gravel of the drive.

Her room, the room she had occupied when she had lived at the vicarage, was a small room at the front of the house, and so she could look down at the long black car without impediment. For a heart-stopping moment she wondered if it was Matt, come to continue his denunciation, but it wasn't. Her aunt and uncle were climbing out of the limousine, and her heart sank abruptly at this obvious obstruction to her plans.

Leaving her case still open on the narrow bed, she hesitated only a moment before going downstairs. Favouring her left foot, she trod the creaking treads of the stairs with some misgivings. But the vicarage was old, and there was no way she could avoid the bald announcement of her presence.

Her aunt and uncle were in the drawing-room, and as Rachel pushed open the door she could hear her aunt's stifled sobs. In spite of everything, she felt incredibly sorry for her. Her aunt was going to miss Barbara a lot, not least because she had always contrived to give her daughter the best, and Barbara's eventual marriage to Matthew Conroy had been the ultimate triumph. Without any other children to compensate them, her aunt and uncle had no one else—which was one of the reasons why Rachel had allowed herself to be persuaded to come here. But she knew now that it had been a mistake, and the malevolent face her aunt turned in her direction only emphasised the fact.

'Er...' Rachel looked towards her uncle, who had risen to his feet at her entrance, and sought for words. 'I—er—I thought I'd be going——'

'Going?' echoed her uncle blankly.

'Going where?' demanded her aunt, with sudden animation.

Rachel moistened her dry lips. 'Um—back to London,' she managed, after a moment. 'Home,' she added, for good measure. 'If I leave now, I should——'

'But this is your home, Rachel.' Her uncle was gazing at her with anxious eyes. 'My dear, have you forgotten already what we were saying as we drove to Rothmere? Don't you see? This is our chance, our opportunity to be reconciled.'

Rachel didn't know what to say. It was certainly not what she had expected, and, looking at her aunt, she still couldn't believe she had any part of this plea for reconciliation.

'Uncle Geoff,' she began awkwardly, 'I do appreciate what you say, but—well, I can't stay here. My work—my friends—are in London——'

'He's not asking you to live here,' broke in her aunt abruptly. Drying her eyes with impatient fingers, she, too, got to her feet. 'But you can't leave—not yet; not tonight. It wouldn't be right. What would people say?'

Rachel was getting a little bit sick of worrying about what other people might say, or think. It was ten years since she had left the area. Ten years since she had had to care what anyone might say or think about her actions. That was one advantage of living in London. She could come and go as she pleased, with no one to feel answerable to. She had got used to being free, uncommitted, and if sometimes she found her life a little empty, it was the price she paid to guard her independence.

'I don't see how my staying on here for another night will silence any speculation,' she said at last, looking at her uncle rather than Aunt Maggie. 'And, as I say, I do have a job——'

'Another night?' exclaimed her aunt, with irritation, and Geoffrey Barnes rubbed his hands together nervously as he was left to explain their wishes.

'We thought—well, that you might stay on over the weekend,' he ventured, giving Rachel a hopeful look, and she sighed.

'But it's only Tuesday, Uncle Geoff. That's *five* more days!'

'Little enough, I should have thought, after what we've done for you,' retorted her aunt bitterly. 'What would you have done all those years ago if we hadn't taken you in, that's what I'd like to know? All those years we gave you a home, and now you can't spare five days to give your uncle and me a little support when we need it.'

'Oh, Aunt Maggie——'

'Maggie, my dear, we don't want Rachel to stay because she feels she owes us something——'

Rachel and her uncle spoke together, but Maggie Barnes was unrepentant. 'Why not?' she demanded, responding to her husband's reproachful words. 'She does owe us something, and if this job of hers was important enough to break up her marriage for, then surely she can take a couple of days off when she feels like it without its causing the whole television station to close down!'

Rachel bent her head. They all knew that the idea that she and Matt had separated because she had been offered a better job in London was just a myth, but this was hardly the time to resurrect those old grievances. And her aunt knew it. That was why she was using it now. Because she knew Rachel wouldn't—*couldn't*—contradict her. Not with Barbara's body lying scarcely cold in its grave.

'We would be grateful if you could stay, of course,' her uncle murmured now, evidently torn between his desire to please his wife and his Christian duty to be fair. 'But only if you feel you can,' he added awkwardly. 'I mean, we'll understand if you have to get back to London.'

Would they? Rachel wondered. She doubted that her aunt would forgive her if she chose the latter course, and, while she might tell herself that subsequent events had destroyed the normal family ties there should have been between them, nothing could alter the fact that they had given her a home when her father had died.

'All right,' she said at last, feeling an undeniable sense of entrapment. 'I'll stay until Sunday. But I'll have to ring Justin Harcourt. He's expecting me back in the office tomorrow morning.'

'Justin Harcourt?' muttered Aunt Maggie scornfully, gathering her bag and gloves together and making for the door. 'What kind of a name is that for a man? *Justin!* I suppose he's one of those left-wing intellectuals, with long hair and Jesus sandals!'

'Nevertheless, he is my boss, and I have to call him,' replied Rachel, biting back the urge to defend Justin to them. The brilliant, bulky editor of *Network Southeast* didn't need any defending, and she was not about to play into Aunt Maggie's hands by extolling the awards he had won for television journalism, or announcing that the programme they both worked on was presently the number one current affairs programme in the UK.

'You can use the telephone in my study,' said her uncle helpfully, more than relieved at her capitulation, and Rachel forced a smile.

'Thanks,' she said, as her aunt made a sound of impatience before disappearing upstairs. 'I'll make the call now.' Then, aware of the clammy after-effects of her exchange with Matt, she added, 'And then I'll take a bath, if you don't mind. I'd like to freshen up.'

Justin was predictably peevish when she told him she wouldn't be back at work until Monday. 'You said two days, Rachel,' he reminded her irritably, and she could hear his pencil beating a tattoo on his desk—a sure sign of his uncertain temper.

'I know I did,' she conceded ruefully, perched on the edge of Uncle Geoff's worn leather armchair. 'But—well,

Barbara was my cousin, and—and I can't just walk out on them.'

'Your aunt and uncle?'

'Yes.'

'The aunt and uncle who've made no attempt to see you in ten years?'

Rachel sighed. 'Yes.'

'Oh, Rachel!'

'Well...' She was defensive now. 'Look, circumstances alter cases. You know that. And—and it's different now, now Barbara's—Barbara's——'

'Dead?'

'Not here,' amended Rachel uncomfortably. 'Justin, she was their only child. It's only natural that they should feel bereft.'

Justin was silent for a moment. Then he said harshly, 'And are you planning on taking your cousin's place? Now that Barbara's dead, do you feel differently about what happened between her and your ex-husband? Have you seen him, by the way? You must have, I suppose. Is he part of this sudden desire to assuage your aunt and uncle's grief? Perhaps you're hoping you can assuage his grief, too?'

'No!' Rachel was incensed at his words. 'That's not true. None of it. To start with, Aunt Maggie would be the last person to want me here, and as for taking Barbara's place—well, I couldn't. I wouldn't want to. My home's in London now. I'm happy there. The last thing I need is for you to start putting ideas like that into Dan's head. Five days more and I'll be back. And that's a promise.'

'I'm sure our inestimable producer will be glad to hear it,' remarked Justin drily. 'But you still haven't mentioned Conroy. How's he taking it? Or would you rather not say?'

'You are a bastard, Justin.' Rachel's fingers clenched around the receiver. 'Matt—Matt's upset, of course.' Or was he? She had seen no evident signs of it. 'And naturally I've see him, and—and spoken to him. It was no big deal. We are civilised human beings. Or, at least, some of us are.'

'All right, all right.' To her relief, Justin appeared to accept her protestations at face value, and Rachel breathed a little more easily. 'OK. So we can expect you back in the office on Monday morning, right? Bright and early, hmm? Just in case we're swamped with mail.'

'Right.'

Rachel made her farewells and replaced the receiver, not realising until after the phone had been put down that she was trembling. It was ridiculous, she thought impatiently. It wasn't as if Justin had been particularly objectionable. On the contrary, if anything, he had been fairly easy on her, and she knew he would intercede with Dan Stern on her behalf. No, her call to Justin was not to blame for her present state of upheaval. She had been on edge ever since yesterday, when she had had that run-in with Matthew and his daughter. And his attitude towards her today in no way reassured her that the past was literally dead and gone.

Sitting comfortably in the bath some fifteen minutes later, however, she was more inclined to dismiss her earlier apprehensions. Lying back in the water, made soft by a little of Aunt Maggie's bath salts, she endeavoured to relax. What were five more days, after all? she asked herself logically. At home, in London, five days could pass incredibly quickly, particularly if she was obliged to work on Saturday mornings too. And spending a few days in such spectacular surroundings ought to be an advantage. She had always loved the scenery of the Lake District, and she could surely put up with her aunt's ill-humour if it meant so much that she should stay.

And, however much she tried to avoid the fact, she did owe her aunt and uncle quite a lot. She had often wondered what might have happened to her if her father's brother and his wife had not taken her in. Twenty years ago, the alternatives of either a foster home or an orphanage had not sounded at all inviting, and she had been unutterably relieved when Mr Jennings, her father's solicitor and the executor of his will, had informed her she was to live with her relations.

All the same, it had been a daunting experience, travelling north to Cumbria to live with an aunt and uncle she had never even met. Her father had been totally unlike his brother, so Mr Jennings had told her. Her uncle had been quite content to enter the Church and live a quiet existence, whereas her father had chosen to help his fellow man in a totally different way. After qualifying for the medical profession, he had taken himself off to Africa, where he had considered his talents could be put to best use. He had married her mother, a nurse he had met working in Nigeria, and for the first five years of Rachel's life Lagos had been her home. Then, tragically, her mother had died in one of the seasonal outbreaks of some intestinal disease that was prevalent in the area, and her father, grief-stricken by his loss, had packed up himself and his small daughter and moved back to England.

But from then on, until his death some six years later, they had never settled in one place for longer than a few months. Her father, once a caring, conscientious physician, had started drinking, and although Rachel was too young to understand all that was happening she soon realised that their nomadic existence and her father's growing dependence on the bottle were linked.

Nevertheless, when he died she was devastated. He was all she had had, and she had loved him very much. She was frightened, too, by the knowledge that, although she was almost twelve years old, and had been taking care of the various apartments and rented houses she and her father had lived in for the past six years, the authorities were not going to allow her to live alone and look after herself.

That was when Percy Jennings, her father's solicitor, had come to her rescue. It was he who located her father's brother and informed him of Philip Barnes's death. Until that time there had been no communication between the brothers—not since before Rachel was born, anyway—and when she was told that he had offered her a home she had known an overwhelming sense of relief. In spite of her father's addiction, her experiences of family life had all been good, and although she had been a little apprehensive on that journey north she had never doubted that she would be made welcome.

Consequently, it had been quite a surprise to encounter hostility in her new home, almost from the first day. It soon became apparent that Geoffrey Barnes's sense of responsibility for his orphaned niece was not shared by his wife and daughter. Aunt Maggie had taken an immediate dislike to her, and Barbara had resented her. From the tentatively happy anticipation of making a new life with her new family, Rachel had sunk into a chasm of despair, and the first few months she had spent at St Mary's vicarage had been the most miserable time of her life.

Of course, she had rallied. She was not her father's daughter for nothing, and she made friends of her own who compensated for her cousin's spitefulness. And Uncle Geoff had always treated her with affection, she acknowledged honestly. The trouble was, he had always seen the best in people, particularly in his own family, and in consequence he'd never known the many minor injustices Rachel was made to suffer.

The water was getting cold now, and, wrapping the rather rough towel which Aunt Maggie had provided around her, Rachel stepped out of the bath. It had all happened a long time ago, she told herself firmly, determining not to brood about the past. Just because she was here, in Rothside, in the vicarage where it had all started, there was no reason to start remembering events that no longer had any bearing on her life.

After ensuring that the landing was deserted, Rachel scuttled back to her room, shivering in spite of the evidence that the central heating had been set in motion. The ancient pipes and radiators were clunking their way into action, filling the old building with odd bangs and clangings. That was a sound Rachel remembered well

from winter mornings, but, aware of the dangers of remembering, she resolutely dismissed the thought.

Matthew stalked down to the stables in a foul mood.
The morning had begun badly, and it showed no signs
of improving. The conversation he had had with his
mother at breakfast had been partly to blame. She was
concerned about Rosemary. She was upset about the way
he had boorishly banished her to bed the previous afternoon. But she could have no idea of the anguish he had
felt when he had found his daughter talking to Rachel.
He had wanted to punish them both. But, of course, he
couldn't do that. So, instead, he had used Rosemary as
a convenient scapegoat and taken his anger out on the
child yet again. He wasn't proud of what he had done.
He had felt bloody awful about it for the rest of the day,
as a matter of fact. Thank God for the anaesthetic ef-
fects of alcohol, he thought broodingly. At least, he had
been able to induce a blessed state of unconsciousness
for a while.

But seeing Rachel again had hit him harder than he
could have anticipated. He found that wounds he had
thought healed and, if not forgotten, at least invisible,
were dangerously vulnerable. She had hurt him—hurt
him badly—and scars like that just didn't fade away.

Of course, his mother suspected what was wrong. That
was why she had intervened. And although, at the time,
he had been furiously angry at her interference, later on
he had acknowledged that it was probably the safest
thing.

Nonetheless, their conversation this morning had been
just as acrimonious. Just because Rachel's name had
not been mentioned, it did not mean it was not upper-
most in both their minds. And then, to cap it all, when
his conscience drove him to find Rosemary and make
amends by taking her over to Ambleside for the day,
once again she was nowhere to be found.

Agnetha had not improved matters, by reporting that
she had found both cigarettes and matches in Rosemary's

bedroom that morning. 'She is very naughty girl, *ja*,' she declared, giving Matthew a winning smile that completely contradicted her words. She fluttered long, feathery eyelashes at him. 'You vish I should help you find her, Mr Conroy? I come with you, *ja*?' Her gaze lingered on his well-formed mouth. 'Ve help each other, no?'

'No.'

Matthew had been curt and abrupt, but he had no time now for Agnetha's flattery. He wasn't a conceited man, but he had been aware for the past six months that the Swedish girl was hoping he might be attracted to her. And the way she was looking at him at this moment convinced him that sooner or later she would have to go. He had put up with it while Barbara was alive. To have given the girl notice would have aroused too many awkward questions, and Barbara had been hysterical enough as it was. But now Barbara was gone. He had no further reason to procrastinate. And it was only his impatience to find his daughter that prevented him from telling her there and then.

The lake lay beneath a mantle of grey vapour, and, in spite of his knit shirt and hacking jacket, Matthew shivered. Yet it was the time of year that he liked best, when the high peaks still carried a cap of snow, but down in the valley bluebells made a carpet beneath his feet.

There was so much colour, he reflected, reluctantly diverted by his awareness of nature. Daffodils and tulips still grew beneath the copse of silver birch and cypress trees that screened the stable block from the house, and almond and cherry blossom sprinkled the paths that led into the cobbled yard. And a dusky pink clematis would soon be growing over the wall of the stables, its delicate flowers sheltered from the winds that blew from the west.

Jim Ryan, his head groom, was just emerging from a barn as his employer strode into the yard. The diminutive Irishman had worked for Matthew, and his father before him, for almost forty years, and although he was in his late fifties now he was still as spritely as ever.

'Morning, Mr Matt,' he saluted the younger man cheerfully, in much the same way he used to address Matt's father when he was alive. 'It's a dull day. Are you thinking that it's likely to get out?'

'Let's hope so.' Matthew's response was crisp, his eyes intent as he glanced round the yard. He acknowledged the shouted greeting of a boy curry-combing a bay mare in the middle of the yard, and thrust his hands into his pockets as he surveyed the surrounding stalls.

'Would you be wanting Saracen saddled?' enquired Ryan tentatively, sensing his employer's mood and not wishing to draw attention to it. 'Sure, and he'd be glad of the exercise, wouldn't you know?'

Matthew expelled his breath slowly. 'Is Rosemary here?' he asked after a moment. 'I thought she might be.'

'The little one?' The Irishman frowned and shook his head. 'No, sir. I haven't seen the young lady this morning, I'm afraid. You'll be looking for her, then?'

'As you say.' Matthew took another breath, trying to control his irritation. Where the hell was she? She ought to know better than to go wandering off. And if she wasn't riding her pony, had she cut across the fells to Rothside yet again?

'Would you have me send young Peter over there to help you?' Ryan was asking now, but Matthew shook his head.

'No,' he said shortly. And then, realising he was being boorish, he softened his words with a slight smile. 'No, I'll find her. Thanks for your help, Jim. I'll let you know if there's anything you can do.'

Striding back towards the house, Matthew remembered he hadn't asked Jim Ryan about the cigarettes, but he decided that could wait. Besides, it was hardly likely that one of his stable-boys would have given them to her. He thought they had more sense, particularly as they knew they were not indispensable, and it would hardly be worth risking dismissal for such a ridiculous offence. No, Rosemary had to be getting them from somewhere else. But where? Agnetha didn't smoke, so he couldn't blame her.

Fifteen minutes later he was behind the wheel of the Range Rover, on his way to the village. None of his staff knew where Rosemary was, and he was rapidly losing patience with the whole affair. All the same, he couldn't help remembering his daughter's face when he had bawled her out the previous day. He hoped to God she hadn't done anything really rash, like thumbing a lift into Penrith or Carlisle. She was reckless enough to do it, and his anger was tempered now with an unwilling sense of anxiety.

He was halfway along the lake shore when he saw them. A mile beyond the gates of the estate the road dipped down towards the lake, and in summer tourists parked above a shingly stretch of beach, and launched windsurfers and dinghies into the shallow water. Presently, however, it was too early for holiday-makers, during the week at least, and the woman and child who were exploring the rocky inlet were completely unaware of anyone's observation.

For a moment, Matthew was almost blinded by the anger he felt at seeing them together yet again. Then, without even thinking what he was doing, he stepped on his brakes, bringing the Range Rover to a screeching halt in the middle of the road, only realising his mistake when a van behind set up a noisy protest.

'Blast!'

Raising a hand to placate the driver behind, Matthew thrust the vehicle violently back into gear and drove it on to the parking space above the beach. Instead of being able to come upon his daughter and her companion unawares, the noisy horn-blowing had drawn their attention to his ignominious arrival, and when he climbed from behind the wheel Rosemary already looked as if she was on the point of taking off.

But it was the woman who took the initiative. As if assessing Rosemary's feelings, she took the little girl by the hand and faced him with cool condemnation, her green eyes meeting his without any trace of intimidation.

'Were you trying to frighten us?' Rachel enquired coldly, as Matthew strove to regain his composure. 'Was it absolutely necessary to make such a noise? We're not blind. We would have seen you, sooner or later.'

Matthew's jaw clamped. 'It wasn't my fault,' he declared, between his teeth. 'What do you take me for? Some kind of moron? I stalled the car, that's all. Someone else blew their horn.'

Rachel regarded him doubtfully. 'Then who was it?'

'The idiot behind,' retorted Matthew, not altogether charitably. It had been his fault, after all. He took a steadying breath. 'Might I ask what's going on?'

'Rachel's been showing me how to play ducks and drakes,' put in his daughter quickly, evidently feeling confident enough to loosen her hand from Rachel's. 'Look!' She bent and picked up a flat pebble, and made an amateurish attempt to send it skimming across the water. 'Rachel says you used to be good at it. Were you, Daddy? Were you? Will you show me?'

The child's prattle had given Matthew time to gather his thoughts, however, and his initial anger at finding his daughter with the woman he had believed would be safely back in London hardened.

'Never mind about that, how dare you leave the estate again without my permission?' he demanded fiercely, catching the child's arm in a purposeful grasp and jerking her swiftly towards him. 'Do you realise I've spent the past hour looking for you?'

'Daddy!'

Rosemary's cry was painful, but Matthew was in no state to care if he was hurting her. His own feelings were too raw and chaotic to pay much attention to his daughter's.

'For goodness' sake——'

Rachel was evidently shocked by his behaviour, but Matthew hardly cared what her reaction might be. 'It didn't occur to you that people might be worried about her, did it?' he snarled. 'After all the publicity there's been about children wandering off on their own, and being picked up by some pervert, you happily let her stay with you, indifferent to any upheaval it might be causing.'

Rachel stiffened now. 'You can hardly pretend that it's the first time,' she stated, aware of Rosemary's anxious eyes upon her, and Matthew scowled.

'Whether it is or not is no concern of yours,' he retorted. 'The fact remains, you didn't give a——' He broke off at this point and rephrased his statement. 'You didn't *care* that her absence might create a panic. It's bad enough that you should be the one to find her, without——'

'I didn't know that you were looking for her!' Rachel interrupted him abruptly. 'And it's not been my impression that you particularly care where she is, in any case.'

Matthew's free hand balled into a fist. 'And what would you know about it?' he demanded, as Rosemary started to squirm about in an effort to free herself. 'As far as I know, you've only met my daughter on one other occasion——'

'Two other occasions,' Rachel corrected him swiftly. 'We spoke together yesterday, remember? Before you ordered her off to bed!'

Matthew was incensed. How dared this woman stand there and accuse him of ignoring his daughter's needs, when she had never had a child of her own and obviously knew nothing about children. She hadn't even *wanted* a child, he remembered, with bitter loathing. All those months, when he had hoped she might get pregnant and she had been using a contraceptive. The memory was painful; it exposed an unprotected nerve.

He stepped towards her then, infuriated enough in that instant to do her some physical injury, and, sensing her father's distraction, Rosemary chose that moment to break free. With a rueful grimace in Rachel's direction, she darted off along the beach, ignoring Matthew's angry summons to, 'Come back here, at once!' and plunging between the trees that edged the lake shore at that point.

There was a moment's shocked silence, while both of them turned to watch Rosemary's departure, but when Matthew would have started after her Rachel stepped into his path.

It was a brave thing to do, even Matthew had to give her that, but he was in no mood to respond to courageous gestures. Rosemary was disobeying him, and at this point it was the final ignominy.

'Get out of my way!' he exclaimed, pushing Rachel aside without compunction, but she was lighter than he had imagined. Instead of making her step back, his hasty propulsion sent her sprawling on to the sand, and there was an ominous thud as her head struck a rock.

'Oh, *hell*!'

His pursuit of Rosemary forgotten, Matthew dropped down on to one knee beside Rachel's now still form and, laying his hand against her neck, he felt the fluttering pulse. Dear God, she was unconscious, he realised sickly. She must have hit her head harder than even he had imagined, and the realisation that he might have caused her some irreparable damage caused his heart to accelerate in horror.

He was hardly aware of Rosemary's return until she, too, dropped to her knees beside Rachel. 'She—she's not dead, is she, Daddy?' she exclaimed, her pale face even whiter than usual as she lifted her head to look at him, and he found himself giving her an impulsive hug of both relief and reassurance.

'No, she's not dead,' he declared, although his mouth was dry as he said the words. 'She's just—lost consciousness, that's all. I think she hit her head when she fell. She'll come round in a minute.'

'How did she fall, Daddy?' the little girl asked, evidently emboldened by his unaccustomed display of affection, and Matthew sighed.

'She just—fell, that's all,' he said, not altogether truthfully. He took off his jacket, and laid it over

Rachel's unconscious form. 'God, I wish she'd open her eyes!'

'I think she's bleeding!' Rosemary burst out suddenly. She pointed to the trickle of blood that was darkening the rocks near Rachel's head. 'Oh, Daddy, she is going to be all right, isn't she? She's not going to die like—like Mummy?'

'I hope not,' muttered Matthew absently, hardly aware of what he was saying as he rolled Rachel's head to one side to expose a small but deep cut at the base of her scalp. Then, realising what he had said, he reached out and squeezed the child's hand. 'No. No, of course she's not going to die,' he repeated, with more vehemence than conviction. 'But we're going to have to get her to a doctor. And quick.'

A tear trickled from the corner of Rosemary's eye. 'You won't let her die, will you, Daddy?' she persisted. 'I liked her. I really liked her. And—and I think she liked me.'

'Don't say *liked*!' For a moment, Matthew's composure slipped. Putting one hand beneath Rachel's neck, and the other behind her knees, he lifted her into his arms. 'You *like* her,' he amended, getting somewhat unsteadily to his feet. 'Present tense. Not past.'

It was doubtful that Rosemary understood what he was saying, but she seemed sufficiently reassured to hurry ahead of him to open the door of the Range Rover.

'In the back, Rosemary,' her father directed, and the little girl swung the rear door open. 'Now, you get in the other side and try and keep her head still. It's going to be a bumpy ride.'

Moving her had caused the wound on Rachel's head to bleed more freely, and the darkening stain on the velour upholstery spread with frightening speed. Giving her one last look, Matthew was forced to get into the driver's seat and take control, but it was difficult to concentrate on what he was doing when his thoughts were all with the woman lying so motionlessly on the back seat.

Dear God, he prayed silently, let her be all right. You know I never intended this to happen.

He drove straight to Rothmere. The house was nearer, and he knew it would be easier for the doctor to come to them than the other way about. Even so, his arrival at the house caused no small upheaval, and the situation wasn't improved when Lady Olivia appeared just as he was carrying Rachel upstairs.

'Matthew!' she exclaimed, gazing up at him from the bottom of the stairs, her eyes wide with accusation. 'In God's name, what is going on?'

'Watkins will tell you,' replied Matthew, not pausing in his ascent. 'Oh, and will you ask Agnetha if she has a nightgown Rachel can borrow? Her sweater and jacket will have to come off.'

'But what has happened?' demanded his mother fiercely, but her son had gone. Matthew, with Rosemary skipping anxiously at his heels, had disappeared along the corridor that led to the west wing.

CHAPTER FIVE

HER head hurt. That was Rachel's first thought. As she stirred on the pillow she felt the restrictive pressure of something that was bound about her head, and when she lifted a curiously weak hand to explore the reasons her fingers encountered the unmistakable fabric of a bandage.

A *bandage*! She blinked, and found that hurt, too. In fact, her whole head ached; so much so that she didn't even have the strength to lift it off the pillow. But what was she doing lying in bed, in the middle of the day, wearing a bandage? It didn't make sense. She hadn't put the bandage on her head, so what was it doing there? Of course, her head did feel as if it was definitely not misplaced, but how had it happened?

And then she remembered. Or at least, she thought she did. She had been down at the lake, playing ducks and drakes with Rosemary; and Matthew had found them...

A sense of dizziness swept over her at this thought, and she gripped the quilt that was covering her with suddenly sweating fingers. But even the quilt was unfamiliar, and when she cautiously opened her eyes again she realised she was lying in a totally unfamiliar bed.

For a moment the room swam before her dazed eyes, but then, unbelievably, she realised where she was. Oh, the room had changed, of course. When she had used it, it had been decorated in shades of cream and lilac, and the floor-covering had been a dusky Aubusson that she had chosen herself. Now the walls were covered with peach silk, and the rug had been replaced with a white pile carpet, but no one could alter the size and dimensions of the room Rachel had occupied when she was

59

eighteen years of age. She was at Rothmere, she acknowledged disbelievingly. But why?

She frowned, trying hard to think, but her brain felt like a sponge. All she was certain of was that it had had something to do with Matthew—and Rosemary. She tried to shake her head and winced. Surely he hadn't attacked her for playing with his daughter?

Her efforts to bring some coherence to her thoughts were arrested when the door of the bedroom opened. She heard the sound, even if she couldn't turn her head to see who had entered. For a moment she was tempted to close her eyes again and pretend to be asleep. There was always the possibility that it might be her ex-husband, come to see how she was, and she didn't think she had the strength to face him right now. But the figure that swam into her vision was not tall enough to be Matthew, and her eyes widened to encompass the uniformed figure of a nurse.

'Ah, you're awake!' she exclaimed, with evident relief. She came towards the bed. 'How are you feeling?'

Rachel moistened her dry lips. 'Thirsty,' she admitted. 'What am I doing here?'

'First things first,' said the nurse, who was younger than Rachel, and very attractive. She slipped a hand beneath Rachel's shoulders, and helped her to take a sip of water from the glass she held in her other hand. 'There. Is that better? I must say, you do have a little more colour.'

Rachel tried to be patient. 'But why am I here?' she protested. 'What happened? What time is it?' Now that she noticed it, the pale sunlight filtering through the half-drawn curtains did seem awfully low. 'My uncle—he'll be wondering where I am.' She shifted agitatedly beneath the nurse's soothing hands. 'Has anyone thought to tell my aunt and uncle where I am?'

'Of course, of course.' The nurse was coolly unperturbed. 'Naturally, your family have been told where you are. Mr Conroy saw to that himself. And I expect they can come and see you later, after Dr Newman has examined you again.'

'*Again?*' Rachel's head was throbbing, but she had to know what was going on. 'What do you mean? Has he examined me already?'

'Has he examined you already?' The young nurse chuckled at her words. 'Don't you remember?'

Rachel swallowed. 'Obviously not.' She tried not to panic at the thought. 'When—when did Dr Newman examine me?'

'At the hospital,' said the nurse firmly. 'In Penrith. You don't remember going to the hospital?'

Rachel made a negative gesture.

'Oh, well——' the girl was unbearably casual about it all '—not to worry. You will. It often happens like that.'

Rachel's hands clenched. 'What often happens?' she demanded unsteadily. 'What happened to me? Please— you've got to tell me!'

'Now, now, don't go getting upset.' At last, the nurse seemed to realise that Rachel was getting really scared. 'You fell. Do you remember that? By the lake?' she prompted. 'You hit your head.'

'By the lake?' Rachel massaged her temple with a shaky hand.

And then it all came back to her. There had been an argument, she remembered that. Or was *argument* too mild a description of the heated exchange she had had with Matthew? In any event, he had been furious, partly because he hadn't known where Rosemary was, and partly because when he'd found her she had been with Rachel. And she hadn't helped matters by goading him into—into what? Surely he hadn't hit her, had he? She thought there had been a moment when she had half expected he might, but then—then something had happened... Yes, that was it. Rosemary had run away, and when she had tried to stop him from going after her, he had pushed her out of the way——

'You do remember, don't you?' The nurse's anxious voice broke into her thoughts and, wincing, Rachel nodded.

'Most of it,' she agreed. 'But I don't remember anything about a hospital. Did—did Matt take me there?'

'Actually, no——' began the girl, and then broke off abruptly as the door opened again, this time to admit a slim, dapper man, with a thin moustache and sideburns.

Dr Newman? wondered Rachel doubtfully, and then felt a sudden return of panic when her ex-husband followed the other man into the room.

'The patient's awake, Doctor.' Unknowingly answering Rachel's unspoken question, the nurse moved back from the bed. 'She remembers what happened—or most of it, anyway. And she's had a drink of water.'

'Good. Good.' The doctor took the nurse's place at Rachel's bedside, and took her limp wrist between his fingers and thumb. He smiled at her as he took her pulse, and then replaced her arm on the quilt and folded his hands together. 'So—Miss—Mrs Conroy, how does your head feel?'

Conscious of Matthew standing behind the doctor, listening intently to everything that was going on, Rachel found it difficult to speak audibly. 'Um—sore,' she managed, after a moment. And then, clearing her throat, she added, 'When can I go home?'

'Well, not yet,' declared Dr Newman frankly, casting a swift glance over his shoulder at Matthew. 'You've had a mild concussion, Mrs Conroy. I recommend that you stay where you are for at least the next twenty-four hours. Then we'll see.'

'Twenty-four hours?' Rachel was horrified. 'But—I can't.'

'Why can't you?'

Matthew spoke for the first time, coming round the doctor to look down at her with a dark, enigmatic gaze, and Rachel licked her lips. 'Because I can't!' she exclaimed, looking at the doctor and not her ex-husband. 'Dr—Newman, is it?' And at his nod, 'I don't know what you've been told, Doctor, but I have to get back to London on Sunday.'

'In three days' time?' Dr Newman shook his head. 'I don't think so, Mrs Conroy.'

'Three days' time?' Rachel was confused. 'No, not in three days' time. Today's Wednesday——'

'I'm afraid it's Thursday, Mrs Conroy,' the doctor corrected her gently. 'You were unconscious for over twelve hours.'

'Tw—twelve hours!' Rachel's head was pounding now. 'No. No, I can't have been——'

'You were,' said Matthew, with rather less vehemence. 'Believe it.'

Rachel could feel the hot prick of tears behind her lids now. This couldn't be happening, she thought wildly. She couldn't have lost a whole day! It wasn't possible.

'Besides which, you lost a great deal of blood, Mrs Conroy,' Dr Newman was continuing steadily. 'You cut your head, you see. If Mr Conroy hadn't had the foresight to bring you straight to Rothmere, it might have been a great deal more serious.'

'No——'

'I'm afraid it's yes,' declared the doctor firmly. 'Your local doctor was able to stanch the bleeding until an ambulance could be sent out from the Infirmary, and you were in a stable condition by the time you reached the hospital.'

Rachel could hardly take it in. 'I don't remember,' she murmured blankly. 'I don't remember anything after—after——'

'After I knocked you down,' Matthew finished for her tersely. 'Don't worry. I've told the doctor what happened. It was all my fault.'

Rachel steeled herself to look up at him then. 'I fell,' she said distinctly. 'You didn't knock me down. I stumbled, that's all. I—someone stood on my foot yesterday—I mean, on Wednesday—and it must have buckled when I put my weight on it.'

Matthew's mouth tightened. 'If you say so,' he essayed stiffly. 'In any event, you're staying here until you're fully recovered.'

Rachel wanted to protest. She wanted to say that Rothmere was the very last place she wanted to be, and that no one, least of all his mother, would welcome her being here. Aunt Maggie, for one, would be furious. She'd see it as a deliberate attempt to insinuate herself into Matthew's life again.

'I think Mr Conroy is right, you know,' said Dr Newman now. 'Wounds to the head should never be taken lightly, and, no matter how important it is for you to get back to London, you would be extremely foolish to risk your health in that way. My opinion is that you should spend at least one more day in bed, and even then you'll find that getting up is not as easy an option as you seem to think.'

Rachel caught her lower lip between her teeth. 'But—couldn't I go back to the vicarage?' she ventured, but even before Matthew voiced his objections she had realised how impractical that would be. Aunt Maggie might not like her staying at Rothmere, but she certainly wouldn't welcome taking the responsibility upon herself.

'There simply aren't the facilities at the vicarage that there are here,' Matthew informed the doctor impatiently. 'And Rachel knows it. She—well—I imagine she feels it's hardly suitable that she should be staying here, in the circumstances, but——'

'You mean because your wife has just died?' suggested Dr Newman thoughtfully, and Matthew nodded.

'That, of course, but also because of our past—relationship.'

'I see.' The doctor nodded now. 'Well, I'm sure that, the present circumstances being what they are, no one could doubt the veracity of Mrs Conroy's presence.'

'No.' Matthew inclined his head in assent. 'Do you agree, Rachel?'

Her lower lip trembled, and she bit on it hard to disguise the obvious weakness. 'Do—do I have a choice?'

she responded tautly. She determinedly looked at the doctor. 'And—how long do you expect me to be—inactive?'

'Mmm ...' He frowned. 'Well, shall we say—two weeks?'

'Two weeks?'

Rachel fairly squeaked the words, and he gave her a rueful smile. 'At the very least, I would say,' he declared firmly. 'I'm sorry, Mrs Conroy, but I really don't see you withstanding any mental strain for some time.'

By the next morning Rachel had learned enough about her condition to realise that Dr Newman's prognosis had not been as exaggerated as she had thought. Her strength, which she had thought was lying dormant while she was in bed, had simply deserted her, and it was frustrating to find that she really was as helpless as a baby. Even sitting up to swallow some of the chicken broth that Mrs Moffat had prepared for her left her feeling weak and shaky, and she didn't argue when the nurse, whose name she had learned was Linda Douglas, insisted Rachel didn't attempt to get out of bed when she wasn't there.

'Don't worry,' she said, when Rachel expressed anxiety at her own helplessness. 'You'll be surprised how much better you'll feel in a few days. What really upsets your system is the shock. Once you've had time to get over that, you'll find your strength will return fairly rapidly.'

'I hope so.' Rachel spoke with urgency. 'As soon as I can, I'd like to return to the vicarage.' She caught her lower lip between her teeth. She could just imagine what a juicy item of scandal this was providing for the gossiping tongues of Rothside.

The nurse made no comment as to when she might be able to leave Rothmere, but Rachel was determined to make it sooner, rather than later. In all honesty, she planned to return to London as quickly as possible, convinced that any recuperation that was needed could be accomplished equally as well in her own home.

But she would have to speak to Justin again before Monday. She frowned. What day was it? Thursday? No, Friday. Her calendar was twenty-four hours out of date. Which meant she must speak to Justin the day after tomorrow. She sighed. She dreaded telling him she wouldn't be returning as she'd promised. Like her Aunt Maggie, he would probably think she had engineered the whole thing.

She should never have told him about her relationship with Matthew, she reflected ruefully. In his opinion, Matthew was a selfish bastard who deserved everything that was coming to him, and Rachel had done the only thing possible in getting a divorce.

Of course, when she had related the whole story to him it had been over a drink at the end of a particularly long and arduous day, and she had held nothing back. It had been soon after she'd moved to London, while she was still feeling raw and betrayed, and she had cried very easily in those days. But he had been so sympathetic, and she had badly needed a shoulder to cry on.

Naturally, she had got over it—eventually. But the trouble was, Justin still remembered how distressed she had been then. And when she had asked him for time off to attend Barbara's funeral, he had initially refused permission. Only her avowed intention of going anyway had swayed his judgement, but subsequent events would only reinforce his original impression.

Dr Newman arrived to examine his patient just as Nurse Douglas was helping Rachel back from the bathroom. Dressed in only the flimsy polyester nightdress Matthew's au pair had lent her, Rachel couldn't help feeling rather exposed, and this sensation was made all the more embarrassing when Matthew again followed the doctor into the room.

With scarlet cheeks, Rachel stumbled hastily into the bed, dragging the covers over her trembling form. Who the hell did Matthew think he was, walking into her room unannounced? she thought indignantly. It wasn't as if he had any right to be here. He wasn't a doctor, and he wasn't a friend. He was simply a man she had once been foolish enough to marry, and it had to be said—if it weren't for him, she might not now be in this ignominious position.

'Well,' said Dr Newman, after the nurse had hastily straightened the covers Rachel had so untidily hauled over herself. 'And how are you feeling this morning?'

Rachel wished she could say she felt much better. She wished she was able to announce she was well enough to get up out of the bed, and leave Rothmere before anything more disastrous happened. But she couldn't.

'Tired,' she admitted instead, avoiding Matthew's careful appraisal. 'I don't think I slept awfully well last night.'

'No.' Dr Newman did not sound too surprised. 'Well, I think we should have a look at your head, don't you? Perhaps I can do something to make you feel a little easier.'

Rachel nodded. 'All right.'

But her eyes moved to Matthew, and, as if sensing her reaction to the other man's presence, Dr Newman turned his head. 'I think it might be as well if you left us, Mr Conroy,' he declared smoothly. 'You can come back when we've finished. I think Mrs Conroy would prefer it.'

There was a pause when Rachel half thought Matthew was going to protest, but then, with a brief nod of his head, he departed. But not before Rachel had noticed how Nurse Douglas's eyes followed him from the room.

Removing the dressing from her scalp was painful, and, lying with her face buried in the pillow, Rachel was hardly conscious of the muffled exchange going on between the nurse and the doctor. She didn't know how big the cut was, but it felt enormous, and she wondered if they had shaved her head around the injury. She wanted to groan. Things just seemed to get worse and worse. How would she look with a bald patch behind her ear? she fretted. If only she hadn't gone for a walk on Wednesday morning. If she'd not had that argument with Aunt Maggie over borrowing her rubber boots and walked out of the house, none of this would have happened. She should have stuck to her guns and gone back to London on Tuesday night, as she had intended. She could bet Aunt Maggie was wishing she had, too.

'There we are.' While she had been thinking of other things, the dressing on her head had been renewed, and Dr Newman assisted her back on to her pillows with gentle hands. 'Does that feel easier? You must tell me if it doesn't.'

Rachel winced as her movements caused her head to throb, but it did feel less rigid. 'Yes,' she murmured. 'Yes, it does feel a bit better.' She frowned. 'There's no problem, is there?'

'Not really.' Dr Newman smiled, but Rachel didn't like the qualification.

'Not really?' she echoed. 'Does that mean there is? I'd really rather know, Doctor. Please don't keep me in suspense.'

Dr Newman sighed. 'I'm not. Believe me. It's just that—well, with wounds of this kind there can be complications.'

'What kind of complications?'

Rachel was anxious, and, shaking his head, the doctor seated himself on the side of her bed. 'It's nothing serious,' he assured her. 'Just a little swelling around the wound, that's all. I'm sure that by tomorrow it will have disappeared. But for the moment I'm going to ask Nurse Douglas to give you an antibiotic, just to be absolutely sure. All right?'

Rachel bit her lip. 'If you say so.'

'I do.' He smiled again, and rose to his feet. 'And now I think you should rest. I'll tell Mr Conroy that I don't think you should have any visitors just now.'

Rachel was grateful for his understanding, and she was glad to close her eyes for a little while. But when she opened them later and discovered it was already late afternoon, she felt a helpless sense of panic. It was frightening to realise how little control she had over herself at the moment.

She looked about her, and found she could do so without encountering the throbbing pain that had previously accompanied any movement of her head. She could even lever herself up on to her pillows without any attack of dizziness, and although the effort tired her it was definitely an improvement.

She wished Nurse Douglas had been there to see it, but the young nurse was not in the room. Perhaps she was downstairs talking to Matthew, thought Rachel cynically, recalling the revealing look the girl had cast in his direction. Matthew had always had that effect on women, she remembered, unwillingly aware that the knowledge still had the power to scrape a nerve.

She sighed frustratedly, not really wanting to entertain thoughts of that kind. It shouldn't matter to her what Matthew did, or with whom. He wasn't her concern any longer. If he found Nurse Douglas attractive—so what? All she wanted to do was go to the bathroom. That was more important to her than speculating about Matthew's present sexual activities.

Remembering the nurse's admonition that she shouldn't attempt to get out of bed without assistance, she lay for a few more minutes, waiting for Nurse Douglas to return; but she didn't. And the situation was getting quite desperate. Short of hammering on the floor, there was no way she could attract attention, and as she knew this suite of rooms was in the west wing, and remote from the more regularly used rooms on the ground floor, that means of attracting notice was not very practical.

Deciding she would have to disobey instructions, after all, she weakly pushed back the covers and slid her legs over the side of the bed. Her head swam a little as she pulled herself upright, but she was relieved to find she felt a little stronger than she had done earlier in the day.

Gaining a little confidence, she tested her weight before getting to her feet, and then looked across the room at the bathroom door, in much the same way as a mara-

thon walker might view the winning post. It was only a
few yards, she told herself firmly. And it wasn't as if she
was an invalid. All she had done was cut her head, for
goodness' sake!

The filmy nightgown billowed about her as she pains-
takingly made her way across the floor. Just a few more
steps, she breathed encouragingly, letting go of the rail
of the bed to totter the few steps to the bathroom door.
With her hand clasping the handle, like a lifeline, she
looked back towards the bed with a feeling of disbelief.
Had she really come so far? she thought, aware of the
film of sweat that had broken out all over her body.
Dear God, she hoped Nurse Douglas would come to help
her back to bed. She really didn't think she could make
it on her own.

All the same, it was a great relief to gain her objective,
and afterwards she leant over the basin, dousing her hot
face with cool water. She felt hot and shivery all at the
same time, and her legs were like jelly as she straightened
up and reached for the towel.

The sound of the bedroom door being opened reached
her as she was folding the towel back on to its rail. The
relief she felt was tremendous, and, supporting herself
with the door-frame, she moved to show herself. 'I'm
here,' she was saying wearily, quite prepared for Nurse
Douglas to be angry with her, but it wasn't Nurse
Douglas who had come into the bedroom; it was
Matthew.

The sight of his tall figure, dark and disturbing in black
jeans and a matching black silk shirt, was like a body
blow. He was the last person she had expected—or
wanted—to see in her present condition, and she swayed
against the woodwork, wondering how she was going to
make it to the bed now. Why couldn't it have been Nurse
Douglas? she fretted. All she really wanted was to crawl
back between the sheets.

'You ought not to be out of bed,' said Matthew
abruptly, dropping whatever it was he had been carrying

and starting across the room towards her. 'Where's Nurse Douglas? Does she know what you're doing?'

'Don't—don't come any nearer!' exclaimed Rachel weakly, lifting one trembling hand and holding it out in front of her. She had just remembered the scarcity of what she was wearing, and, while modesty was of little importance in her present situation, she still had some pride left.

But Matthew ignored her. Brushing her protest aside, he swept her up into his arms and carried her back to the bed. Then, after settling her against her pillows, he drew the soft quilt about her.

It was a relief, she had to admit it, but that didn't prevent an automatic sense of outrage. This ought not to be happening, she thought, staring up at him frustratedly. They were divorced, for God's sake! His second wife had just died! And yet she could still feel the strength of his arms about her, and the heated warmth of his body had been unbearably familiar.

'Are you all right now?' he enquired, as she fumbled for a tissue to blow her nose, and Rachel nodded cautiously.

'I'd have managed,' she muttered, avoiding his eyes, and concentrating instead on the creamy wisp of paper he had rescued for her from its box. 'What are you doing in here anyway? I didn't realise my being an invalid in your house gave you the right to walk into my bedroom unannounced!'

'You should be glad I did,' said Matthew shortly, folding his arms across his chest as if to control some latent desire he had to retaliate in kind. 'What were you doing exactly? You've got water all down the front of your nightdress.'

Rachel felt her cheeks reddening, and was furious. For heaven's sake, she was far too old to start blushing again. But a covert examination of her nightgown proved that he was not lying and, to add to her embarrassment, in places the damp material was clinging to her breasts.

Drawing the quilt even higher, she said tersely, 'I was washing my face and hands. I didn't realise I'd splashed myself. Thank you for drawing my attention to it.'

'Don't be ridiculous!' Matthew's mouth compressed. 'I just can't imagine why you couldn't have waited until Nurse Douglas came back. You looked to be on the point of collapse when I came in.'

'Well, I wasn't.' Rachel knew she was being ungrateful, but she couldn't cope with Matthew right now.

'If you say so.' His features hardened. 'But for goodness' sake stop behaving as if I'd never seen you in the nude before——'

'I'm not in the nude!'

'No.' But his expression said as good as. 'Even so, I have been married for a great number of years. The female form is no great novelty, believe me!'

Rachel gave him a bitter look. 'Oh, I do,' she countered tautly. 'So—do you mind telling me what you're doing in my room?'

Matthew sighed, and turned to pick up the object he had dropped when he had charged across the room earlier. 'I collected your things,' he declared, setting the small suitcase on the padded ottoman at the foot of the bed. 'I thought you might prefer to wear your own nightdress.' He paused, and then added grimly, 'Your attitude makes me wish I'd never bothered.'

'Oh.' Rachel didn't know what to say. Contrition warred with self-justification, but the former won. 'I'm sorry.'

'So you should be!' Matthew spoke vehemently at first, but then, as if prepared to give her the benefit of the doubt, he shook his head. 'It wasn't easy, you know,' he went on. 'Your aunt wasn't exactly pleased to see me. Not when I told her why I was there. I think she's wishing you had decided to go straight back to London. Your being here—well, you can guess how she feels.'

'And she's right,' murmured Rachel ruefully, shredding the tissue between her fingers. 'I shouldn't be here——'

'You didn't have a lot of choice,' retorted Matthew drily. 'And it was my fault, after all. Besides, surely we can deal with this like civilised adults? It's not as if your being here can hurt Barbara now.'

'No.' But his reference to Barbara was unsettling, just the same. How had he really felt about her cousin? she wondered. And why had she started asking herself that question, when the answer could be of no interest to her?

'So,' he said, after a moment, 'how are you feeling? Um—Maggie and Geoff are coming to see you tomorrow. Your—er—your uncle sent his best wishes.'

'Thank you.' Rachel caught her lower lip between her teeth. She was not looking forward to seeing either her aunt or her uncle, but she could hardly tell him that. Indeed, she found it incredibly difficult to say anything to him in her present position, and, remembering how she had stood up to him by the lake, she marvelled at her own audacity.

'You scared me half to death, you know,' he added suddenly, his hands falling to his sides, and her pulses quickened at the violence in his voice. Until that moment his attitude had not led her to believe that what had happened had affected him very deeply, but suddenly there was an element of raw emotion in the room. 'I thought I'd killed you,' he continued, pushing his hands into the back pockets of his jeans. 'You'd be amazed how that focuses the mind!'

Rachel could not let him go on. She didn't want to know what it had focused his mind on, and, striving for something to say, she thought of his daughter. 'Did— did you find Rosemary?' she asked, rather inanely, as he was unlikely to be standing here talking to her if the child was still missing, and, although he frowned at the obvious *non sequitur*, he eventually nodded.

'She came back,' he said briefly, lifting his shoulders, and then letting them fall as he breathed out again. 'Believe it or not, she was worried about you.'

'Was she?' Rachel's lips lifted. 'I'd never have believed it.'

'No.' Matthew's eyes were disturbingly intent. 'Are you going to tell me why?'

'No.' Rachel sighed. 'I don't think so. Not right now, anyway.'

Matthew tilted his head. 'That presupposes that we'll be talking to one another again,' he pointed out evenly, and she forced herself to look up at him.

'And won't we?' she challenged, meeting his eyes for the first time, and he actually smiled.

'Maybe,' he agreed. 'If that's what you want.'

'I'm in your house, Matt,' she told him tersely, not quite having got the answer she had expected. 'What I want doesn't come into it.'

Matthew's smile disappeared. 'You don't have to adopt that attitude, Rachel. I thought we were beginning to communicate at last.'

'Communicate?' Rachel almost choked on the word. 'Yesterday—no, two days ago—you were practically foaming at the mouth because I was playing with your daughter.'

'That's an exaggeration!'

'Is it?' Rachel's nails dug into her palms. 'I thought that was how I came to be here.'

Matthew scowled. 'That was below the belt!'

'Yes. Yes, it was.' Rachel shifted a little desperately against the pillows. If he didn't go soon, she was going to humiliate herself completely by bursting into tears. But she didn't want Matt to be kind and considerate. She didn't want him to offer her sympathy and conciliation. She felt much safer when he was looking at her as he was now.

'So—do I take it you don't want to see me again?' he enquired harshly, taking his hands out of his pockets and balling them at his sides, and she closed her eyes against the treacherous desire she had to reach out and touch him.

'I—just think I'm rather—tired,' she got out unsteadily. 'Thank—thank you for getting my things. I do appreciate it.'

'No problem,' he responded, the clipped detachment in his voice eloquent of his feelings. 'I'll tell Nurse Douglas you want to rest, shall I?'

'If—if you would.'

Rachel opened her eyes again, and for a heart-stopping moment she caught his brooding gaze. And it was electric. The look that passed between them owed nothing to the conversation they had just had. Indeed, it might never have been. There was such a searing intimacy in that exchange that, in spite of the fact that she was lying down, her lower limbs went weak.

And then it was gone, as quickly as it had appeared. Like a fire that was suddenly extinguished, his lids descended, and she was left with the uncanny suspicion that she had imagined the whole thing.

Wishful thinking, she thought bitterly, as the door closed behind him. But why? *Why?* Why, after all these years, was she even considering that she might have made a mistake by walking out on him...?

CHAPTER SIX

RACHEL was seventeen when she first met Matthew Conroy.

Although she would have liked to have stayed on at school and taken her A level examinations, her cousin Barbara, who was nine months her senior, had left school at sixteen, and naturally it was expected that Rachel should do the same. After all, she had no money of her own to support her, and it wasn't fair that her aunt and uncle should bear the burden of her education for a further two years.

So, instead of staying on at the comprehensive school, she got herself a job in Penrith, and enrolled at night-school. Of course, it wasn't always easy getting home from Penrith after the classes, particularly during the winter months, when the roads around Rothside became icy or snow-bound. But she was determined to finish the course, and the encouragement of her tutors more than made up for any disparagement she received at home.

Barbara hadn't yet got a job, considering the kind of employment Rachel had settled for to be beneath her. Manning the check-out at a supermarket was not something she would even consider, and ultimately her parents were prevailed upon to send her to a private secretarial college.

Meanwhile, Rachel was working hard to pass her examinations. But it wasn't always easy, when the supermarket didn't close until eight o'clock in the evening, and she had then to go home and tackle an analysis of one of Arthur Miller's plays. On the evenings when she had a class, and finished early at the supermarket, she didn't go home at all between leaving work at five-thirty and attending night-school at seven. In consequence, during those winter months, she was chilled to the bone by the time she got to the night-school, her fingers so cold they could hardly hold a pen.

Oh, she went into a cafeteria for part of the time, but there was a limit to the length of time one could make a burger and a mug of coffee last, and the proprietor of the café grew to regard her continued presence with a jaundiced eye.

Then, one evening, she missed the last bus home. It wasn't her fault. Immersed in a discussion of the war poets, she hadn't noticed the build-up of snow against the windows of the college, and it wasn't until she emerged and found it lying several inches deep that she discovered what had happened. Because of the conditions, the bus service had had to be suspended, and Rachel was left with the unhappy realisation that she was stranded.

What was worse, all her friends from the college had dispersed by the time she came hurrying back from the bus station. They were used to her dashing away as soon as classes were over, and no one wanted to hang about on a night like this.

Endeavouring to suppress the sense of panic that gripped her as she contemplated the seriousness of her situation, Rachel tried to think positively. There were always taxis, of course, she acknowledged steadily, if she had had the money to pay for one, which she didn't. Or she could walk the seven and a half miles to Rothside. But, given the conditions and the fact that it was dark, that was hardly a credible alternative. And yet what else could she do?

She thought, at first, that the man emerging from the college buildings at that moment was her English tutor. In the faint light filtering from the few windows that were still illuminated, and with snow driving into her face, it was a reasonable error. But as soon as she hurried across the car park she realised her mistake. Mr Evans was not as tall as the man presently turning up his collar against the cold, and when her quickened breathing caused him to turn his head and look at her she saw that he was much younger than the English professor. Besides which, she recognised him!

Until that evening, her knowledge of the Conroys had been limited to the glimpses she had had of them about the village. Although her uncle had sometimes visited the house, on one charitable pretext or another, those were not really social occasions. Aunt Maggie had never gone with him, and her aunt's only invitations to Rothmere had been to organise the annual church fête, which was traditionally held in the grounds of the house. In consequence, all Rachel knew about them was what she had heard, and read in the local newspaper, and Aunt Maggie's gossip, which was not always reliable.

Nevertheless, she recognised Matthew Conroy instantly. Only months before she had been among the crowd of sightseers standing outside the village church when his sister had married Gerald Sinclair, and as Matthew had been one of the groomsmen he had been much in evidence. Indeed, his presence had been the cause of much excited speculation from Barbara and her friends, who all regarded him as the local heart-throb.

And he was good to look at, Rachel had to concede, although at this particular minute his appearance was the least of her concerns. The disappointment at discovering he was not Mr Evans, and therefore not someone she could ask to lend her the taxi fare home, was of greater importance, and her face fell when he arched dark brows in her direction.

'I'm—I'm sorry,' she stammered awkwardly, backing away from him. 'I—er—I thought you were someone else.'

'That's a shame!'

Matthew's mouth lifted in a rueful grimace, but Rachel was in no mood to respond to his lazy teasing. She was wondering if there was anyone left in the building whom she could ask to help her, and she didn't even take the time to wonder why he might have been visiting the college.

'I know you, don't I?'

His next words took her completely by surprise, and, dragging her eyes from the lighted windows, she gave him a wry, disbelieving, look. 'Do you?'

She didn't believe him, of course. She was used to boys making passes at her, and, although she didn't consider herself a beauty, she knew green eyes and blonde hair could disguise a multitude of failings. But Matthew Conroy wasn't a boy, he was a man—and definitely a complication she couldn't afford.

'Yes,' he said now, startling her into an involuntary protest. 'You're from the vicarage,' he added, taking the steps to close the gap between them. 'But you're not the daughter, are you?' He frowned. 'You're the niece.'

Rachel caught her breath. 'How do you know that?'

Matthew's lips curved. 'I've got eyes. I've seen you around the village. And you know who I am, too, don't you? Don't pretend. I can see you do.'

'Oh, can you?' Rachel lifted a woolly gloved hand to wipe flakes of snow from her lashes, thinking how ridiculous it was that they should be standing, having this conversation, in a snowstorm.

'Mmm.' Matthew cast a look around the car park. 'Are you waiting for somebody?'

'Um—no.' Rachel took a deep breath.

'So what are you doing hanging about here?' he prompted drily. 'It's late. Oughtn't you to be at home?'

Rachel hesitated. And then, taking the most momentous decision of her young life, she said recklessly, 'I've missed the last bus home. At least, I haven't missed it, exactly—it's been suspended. Because of the weather. I was hoping to find someone to lend me the fare for a taxi. That's why I'm here. I—I don't suppose you would——?'

'Are you serious?' Matthew's lean, dark face mirrored his sudden change of mood, and Rachel swallowed hard.

'Yes——'

'You must be crazy!' He glared down at her with eyes that glittered, even in the gloom. 'You were going to ask a complete stranger for a taxi fare?'

Rachel stiffened. 'I wasn't going to ask a complete stranger!' she retorted. 'If you hadn't—hadn't been here, I had intended to ask my English tutor. That's who I thought you were. But don't worry. I'm sure there's someone else——'

'Wait!' As she would have stalked away, he caught the strap of her haversack and swung her round to face him. 'You mean—you're a member of this faculty?'

Her cheeks flamed. 'If you mean do I take classes here, then yes,' she told him indignantly. 'What did you think? That I was trying to pick you up?'

Matthew heaved a sigh, but he didn't let her go. 'Forget it,' he said abruptly. 'I'll take you home.'

'You won't.' Rachel was too incensed to think sensibly. 'I don't need your assistance, Mr Conroy. Now— if you'll excuse me,' she added, with heavy sarcasm.

'Don't be stupid!' Matthew wound the strap of the bag more securely round his hand. Then, casting a brief glance up at the thickening snow, he went on, 'What makes you think a taxi-driver will risk the journey to Rothside tonight? Remember, he'd have to make the return trip.'

Rachel pressed her lips together, trying not to show how worried she really was. But he had a point. What if no one was prepared to drive her home?

'Why should you be willing to take me home?' she asked at last, and, sensing her acquiescence, Matthew unwound his hand from the plaited denim.

'Why not?' he countered flatly. 'Call it my good deed for the day. Come on. My car's over here.'

She trudged after him to his car, her booted feet moving with some reluctance, in spite of her tacit acceptance of his offer. After all, for all her knowledge of his identity, he was as much a stranger to her as any taxi-driver would have been. And at least with a taxi-driver she would have felt she was paying for his services. What kind of payment might Matthew Conroy exact?

The car, a huge, light-coloured Mercedes, was parked on the college car park, and for the first time Rachel wondered why that should be so. Unless he was taking classes too, she reflected. But that didn't seem likely, bearing in mind that he was reputed to have a university degree from Oxford, or somewhere like that.

'Get in.'

While she had been worrying over his motives, Matthew had unlocked the car and got inside. And now he was thrusting open the door beside her, urging her to join him. The comparative warmth from inside the car swept out to envelop her in its enticing folds, and she swayed a little unsteadily as the snow spun in a spiral about her. But, although she still had reservations, necessity overcame discretion and, taking a determined breath, she stepped into the car.

She tried to slam the door behind her, but it didn't catch properly, and Matthew leant across her to deal with it himself. For a moment, the hard muscle of his shoulder was pressed against her chest, and she was disturbed by the strength of feeling it aroused. None of the youths she had danced with at church socials, or allowed to kiss her in the vicarage porch afterwards, had ever stirred her emotions in quite that way, and her breasts were tingling quite alarmingly when he withdrew his arm.

'Can you fasten the seat-belt?' he enquired, securing his own in place, and Rachel felt the colour invade her cheeks once again.

'I have ridden in a car before,' she retorted, more sharply than was warranted, but she was troubled by her reaction to him and the words were out before she could prevent them.

'OK.' Matthew's response was mild by comparison, and he started the car as she was fumbling for the anchor point. 'I should have known better than to ask. You don't like accepting my help, do you?'

Rachel thrust the clasp home at last, and sank back against the velour upholstery. Then, turning her head sideways, she murmured helplessly, 'I'm sorry.'

'Hmm.' Matthew had reversed out of the parking bay, and was now driving fairly slowly across the car park. The roads would be easier, with the constant movement of traffic to keep them clear, but the college car park was never full in the evenings, and the snow had been allowed to drift. 'You don't have to worry, you know. I almost never get involved with older women!'

For a moment, Rachel didn't understand him, but then, realising he was trying to put her at her ease, she allowed a soft laugh to escape her. 'Nor I with younger men,' she countered, beginning to relax at last. She paused a moment, and then added, 'I do appreciate this, you know, even if it hasn't sounded that way up until now. I could have phoned the vicarage, of course, but—well, I don't think Uncle Geoff would have welcomed turning out on a night like this. And—and who was to know the buses would stop running? You never know, it might not be snowing in Rothside.'

There was a long silence after this statement, and she wondered, somewhat anxiously, what he was thinking. The last thing she wanted to do was imply that her uncle and aunt wouldn't care how—or even if—she got home. It might be true—in Aunt Maggie's case, anyway—but she would never say so. Some things were too personal to share with anyone else.

She turned her head and looked through the window at the driving snow. The car was a cocoon of warmth in a cold white world, and she shifted a little uneasily against the cushioned back of her seat. She wondered what it must be like to take a car like this for granted, and decided that in her world people would always be more important than possessions.

There was some traffic about in Penrith, but by the time they had negotiated its one-way system of streets and emerged on to the dual carriageway that led to the motorway the cars they passed were few and far between. The road to Rothside crossed the M6 just west of Penrith, and then left the A66 a few yards further on to follow the route to Rothmere.

'It's a filthy night,' remarked Matthew at last, as Rachel was racking her brains, trying to think of something to say, and she nodded in relief.

'You—you might have been right about the taxi,' she murmured, settling the haversack more comfortably beside her feet. 'I don't know what I'd have done if I hadn't met you. Do you think they might have allowed me to sleep in the bus station? After all, it wasn't my fault that the service was closed down.'

Matthew glanced her way, and the false illumination from outside the car mirrored his thoughtful expression. He really was a very attractive man, she thought unwillingly, her eyes drawn to his lean, narrow-boned features. Individually, heavy-lidded eyes above a prominent nose and a thin-lipped mouth would not have struck her as sexy, but he was. His skin was dark, as she knew, and although she guessed he would have shaved before leaving home that evening there was already a darkening shadow around his jawline. And his hair, damp now, and sparkling here and there with melting drops of snow, should have looked a mess because it was too long. But it didn't. It brushed his collar at the back, and fell over his forehead in untidy strands—and she had the most ridiculous urge to run her fingers through it and brush it back against his scalp——

'I don't think bus companies work that way,' he was saying now, and it took her a minute to comprehend what he was talking about. A wave of heat swept over her body at the realisation of what she *had* been thinking, and she struggled to find an answer before he noticed something was wrong.

'Um—oh, well, I'd have had to find a hotel room, then, wouldn't I?' she muttered hurriedly, smoothing her damp palms over her knees. 'I'm glad I didn't have to do that.'

'Particularly with no money,' observed Matthew drily, and she pretended to be absorbed in adjusting her seat-belt. 'So—what course are you taking at college? And couldn't you have missed it for one evening?' He shook his head. 'If I were your uncle, I don't think I would have let you go into town tonight.'

'He didn't. That is,' Rachel licked her dry lips, 'I didn't come into town this evening. I—I work in Penrith. I went straight from work to night-school. I'm studying English to A level.'

Matthew's dark brows descended. 'I see.' He hesitated. 'And do your employers pay your expenses?'

'Heavens, no.' Rachel almost laughed now. 'I don't think they'd consider it important to understand Shakespeare, or even twentieth-century literature, if it comes to that.'

'Why? What do you do?'

Rachel sighed. 'I work in a supermarket. At least, until I pass my exams, anyway.'

Matthew was silent for a few minutes, considering her words, and she wondered what he was thinking. Probably that she was very different from the young women he usually associated with, she decided. Particularly Cecily Bishop, whom her aunt said he was going to marry.

'And what do you want to do?' he said eventually, and it took Rachel a minute to realise he was talking about her career.

'Oh—well, I'd like to work in journalism eventually, but the chances of doing that aren't very good around here. There aren't many local papers, you see, and there are dozens of people with the same ambitions as me. In my class alone there are at least four others who'd like to work on a newspaper, and when you consider that newspapers are closing down all the time...'

She was talking too much, and she knew it, but she couldn't help it. It was important that he shouldn't become conscious of her awareness of him, and at least when she was talking she was not staring at his hands on the wheel.

'Journalism,' he echoed thoughtfully now, and she nodded.

'That's right.' She took a breath. 'I like writing, you see. It's the only thing I'm any good at.' She grimaced. 'But I'll probably have to move to London or somewhere like that to find a job.'

'Will you?'

The snow was driving more thickly now, and Matthew set the wipers on a faster speed to keep the windscreen clear. For a while, it took all his concentration to distinguish the outline of the road ahead, the hedges, which were so pretty in summertime, spilling their frozen burden as the car went by.

As they neared the lake, however, it got a little easier. Nearer the water the snow was not lying so thickly, and the dark shadow of the lake was a familiar guide-mark in a totally white landscape. Even Rachel thought she could have found her way along the lake road, and Matthew, who had been born at Rothmere, knew it even better.

'Almost there,' he murmured, as they passed the private drive that led to the Rothmere estate. 'Your aunt and uncle must be worried about you. You don't suppose your uncle might have set out to look for you, do you?'

Rachel shook her head. 'I don't think so,' she replied, knowing that however concerned Uncle Geoff might be, her aunt would not countenance him turning out on a night like this. Besides, she argued reasonably, what was the point of her uncle risking getting stranded in a snow-drift.

'No?'

Matthew was looking at her now, and she was glad he couldn't see the wave of colour that swept up her cheeks at his words.

'I don't think so,' she repeated, avoiding his gaze. 'Oh, look! There's the church. Doesn't it look pretty?'

'Mmm.' Matthew gave the church only a cursory look before bringing the Mercedes to a halt at the gates to the vicarage. But, as Rachel released her seat-belt and bent to pick up her haversack as a preliminary to getting out of the car, he said quietly, 'You didn't tell me your name.'

'What?' She sat back in her seat and looked at him blankly. 'Um—oh, it's Rachel. Rachel Barnes. My father was Uncle Geoff's brother.'

'Yes. I know the relationship,' declared Matthew surprisingly. 'Your father was a doctor, wasn't he? You had no inclination to follow in his footsteps?'

'No.' Rachel shook her head, forbearing to mention that even if she had—which she didn't, luckily—there was no way she could have afforded the years of training needed for such a profession.

A brief spillage of light across the snow-packed drive revealed that someone had peered through the vicarage's sitting-room curtains, and Rachel guessed that her aunt had heard the car. Of course, she wouldn't know what it was doing at the gate, but when her niece appeared it wouldn't take her long to put two and two together. Rachel had been hoping to pretend she had caught the bus, as usual. She was loath to discuss Matthew's kindness with her family. Knowing how her aunt and Barbara could reduce the most innocent of acts to something dirty, she had hoped to keep this experience to herself.

But now, realising that the longer she stayed in the car, the more suspicious her aunt would become, she reached for the handle of the door.

'I—thanks for bringing me home,' she murmured ruefully, guessing he had seen the revealing twitch of the curtains, too. 'You probably saved my life.'

'But not your reputation, hmm?' he remarked lazily, and now she was sure he had seen the betraying glimmer of light.

'Oh——' Rachel lifted her shoulders in what she hoped was a dismissing gesture. 'I—I'm sure my aunt and uncle will be very grateful to you.'

'Are you?' Matthew did not sound convinced, but although sitting here, talking to him, was both pleasurable and exciting, Rachel had the sense to realise it was dangerous, too. He was far too easy to talk to, and, while this might just be an amusing diversion for him, she sensed it could mean more than that to her. And that was just plain stupid!

'I must go,' she said, gathering the haversack to her chest, as if by creating a physical barrier between them she could protect her innocence. Because she *was* innocent compared to him, and she had no intention of making a fool of herself.

'OK.'

He made no demur when she pulled the handle and opened the door, and the still-falling snow made any prolonged farewells impractical. Instead, he just leaned across the passenger seat and said, 'Good luck!' before slamming the door again and driving away.

CHAPTER SEVEN

RACHEL had assumed that that would be the one and only occasion she would get to speak to Matthew Conroy. In the normal course of events their paths simply didn't cross, and even when she'd discovered that his reasons for being at the college that night had been to deliver a guest lecture on computer technology she had had more sense than to imagine it might be repeated. And even if it were, the chances of her running into him again were a million to one.

No, she was quite prepared to accept her aunt's opinion that she had virtually forced him to offer her a lift home, and that she had probably caused her uncle a great deal of embarrassment. In Aunt Maggie's opinion, she should never have gone to the evening class in the first place; as soon as she'd realised the weather was worsening, she should have come straight home. And she was probably right, Rachel decided in the days that followed. But then, Aunt Maggie hadn't wanted her to attend night-school from the very beginning.

And that was that—until the letter arrived.

The plain white oblong envelope was waiting for Rachel when she got home from work a week later. It was obvious that both her aunt and her cousin were curious about the letter, but, assuming that it was something to do with the course she was taking, they allowed her to open it in private. And Rachel was glad that they had when she read what was inside. It was an invitation to attend an interview at the Penrith studios of Kirkstone Television. If the interview was successful, she would be offered the chance to train as a receptionist, with the opportunities of advancement if and when she acquired the necessary qualifications.

With trembling fingers, she turned to the end of the letter, convinced that Matthew Conroy must have had some hand in this, but the signature was disappointingly unfamiliar. Even so, he had to have had something to do with it, she was sure, and her heart palpitated rapidly at the realisation that he hadn't forgotten her.

Her aunt and cousin were predictably pessimistic. Unaware of Rachel's suspicions that Matthew Conroy must be responsible for the invitation, they assumed that the tutor at the college had arranged the whole thing.

'He obviously has no idea how difficult it is to get a job—any job—in television,' remarked Barbara, tossing the letter on to the sofa. 'He probably knows someone who's arranged for you to have an interview, but that's all. It's getting the job that's the hard part. Not being invited to an interview.'

Rachel knew she was right—about the interview, at least. But that didn't stop her spirits from rising. The idea of working in television, in however small a way, was exciting, and her dreams of becoming a journalist could be realised, if she was ever successful enough to join the station news team.

It was six weeks before she saw Matthew Conroy again, and by then she was a trainee telephonist, working behind the desk at Kirkstone Television. Her interview had been successful, and for the past three weeks she had been learning a variety of skills necessary to the job. She hadn't found it hard. Talking to people had never been a problem. And by the time Matthew appeared she had gained more confidence, due in no small part to the clothes allowance which was part of her salary.

Even so, when Matthew walked into the reception area her excitement at seeing him again almost left her speechless. And when later in the day he invited her to have coffee with him, she could hardly get up from her chair and follow him into the boardroom.

Of course, it had been crazy getting involved with him, she acknowledged now, but at the time she had been blind to the possible consequences of her folly. Where

Matthew was concerned, her common sense had seemed to desert her, and although she had known he was engaged to someone else she had convinced herself there was no harm in being friendly. After all, he had been instrumental in getting her this job, she consoled herself, having learned in her first few days at the television station that he was an active member of the governing board.

But in the weeks that followed it had soon become apparent that Matthew's interest in her went beyond the bounds of a casual relationship. It had become obvious when he invited her to go sailing, and, instead of taking her to some public marina, he brought her to Rothmere. She hadn't needed his mother's steely-eyed air of disapproval to know that what he was doing was both foolish and reckless, and that, although there might only be a few years between them in age, there was a world of difference in background.

But it was while they were out on the boat that Rachel had begun to realise just what she was taking on. Matthew might have been only eight years older than her seventeen, but he was inconceivably older in experience. And when, inexperienced as she was, she had stumbled and fallen into the bottom of the yacht, there had been nothing remotely immature about the way he picked her up.

One minute, she was lying in the bottom of the boat, stunned by the sudden transference from perching on the gunwale to being flat on her back, and the next, Matthew had lifted her up into his arms, holding her between his knees as he perched on the cabin roof, his long, hard fingers digging into her bare midriff.

Somehow, she never quite knew how, the cotton shirt she was wearing under her life jacket had separated from the waistband of her jeans, and Matthew's probing fingers took full advantage of the fact.

'Are you all right?' he demanded huskily, his breath warm against her throat, and she could only nod vigorously. 'I'd never forgive myself if I hurt you,' he added, gripping her waist with strangely possessive hands. 'I think I should examine you, just to make sure there are no bones broken.'

'Oh—no. That's not necessary!' She almost choked on the words, but when she met his gaze she discovered he was grinning.

'We're a little old to play doctors and nurses,' he commented wryly, though he still made no attempt to let her go. 'But if you're game, I have no objections. Who's going to be the patient first?'

Rachel didn't know how to respond to him, and, as if sensing her bewilderment, his hands slid from her waist, along her bare arms to her wrists. Then, bringing each of her hands to his lips in turn, he kissed each individual finger, stroking the sensitive pads with his tongue and turning her bones to water.

He let her go then, as if realising he had gone too far, but it was already too late. It was impossible to hide her feelings for him after that, and, although she sensed that Matthew was not so deeply involved, it was obvious he was attracted to her.

Of course, Rachel tried to be sensible. She even asked him about his fiancée who, Barbara had spitefully told her, had been away with her parents for the past three months. But Matthew always changed the subject when she mentioned Cecily. And, although she knew deep down inside her that she was a fool for letting him get away with it, the temptation to ignore the truth was easier by far.

Cecily had come back from Australia at the beginning of June, just as Rachel's aunt and uncle and Barbara were going on holiday. They had always taken a cottage on Exmoor for a couple of weeks every year, and, although Rachel had usually gone with them, this year she wasn't able to. Apart from the fact that it would have been difficult to get time off, when she had only been working at the television station for a few months, her first-year exams at college were looming, and, although Uncle Geoff had been loath to leave her, his wife and daughter had no such reservations.

Barbara made her feelings clear the night before she went away, however. 'Now we'll see how long your job at Kirkstone lasts,' she taunted, coming into Rachel's room as the other girl was getting ready to go to bed. 'Did I tell you Colonel Bishop is a member of the board, too? You can imagine what will happen when he discovers Matthew Conroy has installed his latest girlfriend in reception.'

Rachel made no comment, although the news that Cecily's father was involved with Kirkstone Television wasn't welcome. Nevertheless, since Barbara and her mother had realised that Matthew had had a hand in offering her the interview at the station she had had to suffer many such accusations, and arguing didn't make things easier, it just prolonged the agony.

Still, the news did persuade her that perhaps she was being a fool in allowing her association with Matthew to continue. As Barbara had cruelly informed her, now that Cecily was home again he wouldn't need her any more, and, no matter how painful the truth might be, she had been only a substitute.

So, for the first week her family was away, she avoided seeing him, not answering the phone when she suspected it might be him, and getting the other receptionists to make excuses for her absence if she glimpsed his now familiar car driving into the car park at the station. Her friends were sympathetic. She was a likeable girl, and most of her contemporaries, who had envied her the attention Matthew Conroy had shown towards her, were willing to help. Of course, there were exceptions. Girls like Barbara, who had been jealous of her success all along. But she could stand their sniggering; it wasn't likely to last long.

In the event, it proved easier to avoid him at work than she had thought. Lynn Turner, who worked for Simon Motley, one of the associate producers of the local features programme *Newsreel*, was pregnant, and as she

was having a particularly difficult time with morning
sickness a temporary stand-in was needed. All the girls
who manned the reception desk were offered the chance
to try for the job, but as it entailed working longer hours,
with no obvious advantages, Rachel was the only one to
volunteer. And she got it. In consequence, the next day
she moved on to the floor above, sharing an office with
Simon and his secretary. And the excitement of being
part of actual programme production at last helped in
a small way to assuage the loss of Matthew.

It seemed her affair—if such a word could be used to
describe her relationship with Matthew—was over, and
the long summer days stretched ahead of her, bleak and
lonely. She had had no idea she would miss him so much,
and she was glad her aunt and uncle, and Barbara, were
away as she struggled to contain her grief—it would have
been so humiliating if they had known she cried herself
to sleep at nights. In the morning she could disguise her
puffy eyes with make-up before anyone at the television
station saw her.

The weekend was the worst. There was no *Newsreel*
on Saturday and Sunday evenings, and, although work
did go on on the programme during the weekend, she
was not involved.

Consequently, her spirits were at their lowest ebb on
Saturday evening when Matthew came to the door.
Rachel had been in the kitchen, preparing herself cheese
on toast in lieu of supper, and she hadn't heard the car.
Afterwards, she supposed she should have checked who
her visitor was before so precipitately opening the door,
but she wasn't thinking clearly, and the practicalities of
the situation didn't occur to her.

Therefore it was something of a shock to discover the
man who was causing such an upheaval in her life
standing with his shoulder propped against the
framework of the porch. And she didn't even have the
time to regret the unflattering aspects of her appearance
before he had straightened and stepped inside, closing
the door behind him and forcing her back along the hall.

She thought at first that he was angry, but anger didn't begin to describe Matthew's feelings at that moment. He was simply furious, and as she backed away along the hall she knew a moment's panic.

'What the hell do you think you're playing at?' he demanded, cornering her in the kitchen, where the cheese on her toast was beginning to burn, and she thought uneasily how attractive he was, even when he was angry. It was a warm evening, and he wasn't wearing a jacket, and his dark blue shirt was open at the neck. He wasn't an especially hairy man, but there were hairs at the base of his throat, curling over the opened shirt and glistening with the heat.

'I don't know what you mean,' she answered him now, stretching out a hand to rescue the toast, but he thrust her arm aside. Instead, he turned off the grill, allowing the smoke of the burning cheese to billow into the kitchen, and, grasping her by the wrist, he pulled her after him out of the room.

By a process of opening one door after the other he eventually found the sitting-room, and, dragging her inside, he practically threw her down on to the couch. 'Now,' he said, standing over her, the taut muscles of his thighs barely inches from her knees as she sat there, 'are you going to tell me why you've been avoiding me? And don't pretend you haven't. I'm not a complete fool.'

'Nor am I,' retorted Rachel tremulously, chancing a brief glance up at him, then wishing she hadn't when she met his cold, hard gaze.

'Am I supposed to understand something from that remark?' he countered dangerously. 'Rachel, I'm warning you, my patience is running thin. Either you tell me what this is about, or—or——'

'Or what?' she muttered, hunching her elbows on her knees and cupping her hot face between her palms. 'What can you do to me that you've not already done?'

'You're not serious?' His response was as much bemused now as violent. 'For heaven's sake! What have I done to you, Rachel? I thought we were—*friends*!'

'For how long?' she exclaimed, scuffing at the carpet with her bare toes. 'You know very well that now—now that Cecily's back, you don't need me any more.'

Matthew swore. 'Who told you that?'

'I didn't need to be told.' Rachel wouldn't look at him. 'You know it's the truth, so why don't you admit it?'

'It's not the truth.' With a muffled oath, Matthew came down on the couch beside her, the depression of his weight causing her to tip automatically towards him. But when he would have put his arm about her shoulders she stiffened and pulled away from him.

'You're crazy,' he said frustratedly, and when she would have turned away he put out his hand and grasped her chin, tilting her face towards him. 'Crazy,' he repeated harshly, rubbing his thumb across the vulnerable curve of her mouth. 'I'm not interested in Cecily. I've told you that before.'

'But you're going to marry her anyway.'

'No, I'm not. Why don't you believe me?' He sighed. 'Have I ever lied to you?'

Rachel quivered. 'I don't know, do I?'

'Yes, you do.' Aware that she was weakening, albeit against her will, his hand slid under her chin to cup the gentle hollow of her throat. 'Just because I haven't slept with you yet, it doesn't mean I haven't wanted to.'

Rachel caught her breath. 'I—I wouldn't let you anyway.'

'Wouldn't you?' His eyes dropped sensuously to her lips, and the quickened rise and fall of her small breasts. 'My darling, if that was all I had wanted you wouldn't have been able to stop me.'

'Because you're so irresistible? Is that it?' she retorted, trembling uncontrollably, and he shook his head.

'Just sure of you,' he amended huskily, and, as if unable to control himself, he leant forward and touched her startled lips with his tongue. 'Stop trying to create a situation of contention when there is none,' he whispered, his breath moistening the hollows of her ear. 'And don't pretend you don't want to see me again, or I might not be responsible for my actions.'

Rachel jerked back. 'But what about Cecily?' she persisted, getting abruptly to her feet. 'You won't ever talk about her. Whenever I mention her name, you change the subject.'

Matthew groaned. 'You don't listen, do you?' he declared, and when she turned her back on him he got to his feet, too, and came to stand right behind her. 'What do you want me to say?' he demanded, in a low voice, and she lifted her shoulders as if to ward off an attack. 'For heaven's sake, Rachel, don't make this any harder than it already is! Why can't we just go on as before? What has happened to make you change your mind?'

'Cecily's come back, hasn't she?' she mumbled, her bent head exposing the vulnerable curve of her nape. 'Everyone knows. It's common knowledge in the village. They're all saying you'll be getting married now, and speculating when it's going to be.'

'Oh, *God*!' His plea was heartfelt, and she flinched when his hands descended on her shoulders. 'Cecily's been back in England since the beginning of May. Just because she's not been here, in Rothside, it doesn't mean I haven't been in touch with her.'

Rachel's spine became rigid at his words, but when she would have pulled away he wouldn't let her. Instead, his fingers probed the fine bones that the thinness of her cotton T-shirt could not disguise, kneading and massaging the bunched muscles that her tenseness refused to relax. 'Stop fighting me,' he said, bending his head to brush his lips against the side of her neck. 'Ask me what I was in touch with her about, if you must. It wasn't to arrange a wedding. Quite the reverse, actually.'

Rachel took an unsteady breath. 'Then why has she come back?' she exclaimed.

'This is her home,' replied Matthew evenly. 'Where else would she go? You're not the only one with pride, you know.' He paused. 'And perhaps she's hoping that I'll change my mind.'

Rachel made a disbelieving sound, moving her head jerkily from side to side. 'Why—why should I believe you?'

'Why should you not?' he countered harshly, his hands sliding sensuously down her arms to her elbows. His thumbs brushed the sides of her breasts, and she heard his sudden intake of breath. 'In any case, we shouldn't be having this conversation. Not yet, at any rate. You've still got another year before you finish school.'

Rachel quivered. 'What has that got to do with anything?' she protested, hardly daring to believe what she was hearing, and he expelled a weary breath.

'You *know*,' he muttered unevenly, and then, as if losing all control of the situation, he hauled her back against him. 'I'm trying to be reasonable,' he breathed, against the silky weight of her hair. 'How I've stopped myself from touching you these past few months is beyond me!' His hands slid round her midriff, and rubbed back and forth against the undersides of her breasts. 'I don't want you to feel I'm trying to rush you. I just want us to go on as we were before—before you ruined this otherwise perfectly good week of my life.'

Rachel swallowed. 'And—and what if I don't want to go on as—as before?' she whispered convulsively. 'Wh—what then?'

Matthew dragged her closer, his arms enfolding her against his taut body, and for the first time in her life she felt the unmistakable thrust of a man's arousal. His hardness swelled against her bottom, its heat barely confined by the tightness of his cotton jeans, and a rippling sense of excitement filled her at the realisation that she could do that to him.

'Don't—don't play games with me, Rachel,' he said, and for the first time she heard the harsh edge of emotion in his voice. 'Making me prove that you want me just as much as I want you isn't very sensible. So, if you want to get out of here with your virtue intact, you'd better take that back right now.'

He meant it! *He really meant it!* Rachel's pulses were racing wildly now, and acting purely on instinct, she flexed her shoulders against his chest. The buttons of his shirt felt unbearably sharp against her sensitised flesh, and taking the initiative now, she ran her hands down the seams of his jeans.

'Perhaps you didn't—understand me,' she murmured, and he sucked in some air. 'When I said I didn't want to go on as before, I didn't mean we shouldn't see one another. As you said before—quite the contrary.'

Matthew shuddered then, and for a moment he pressed even closer. But, as if common sense and his own innate sense of decency grimly prevailed, he steeled his aroused body and dragged himself away from her. But not far. With hands that were not quite steady, he turned her to face him, though he carefully kept a foot of space between them.

'You don't understand——' he began thickly, but she interrupted him.

'No. *You* don't understand,' she retorted, her emotive gaze sweeping over his dark, frustrated face, and down over the muscled planes of his body. Her eyes lingered longest at the revealing junction of his thighs, before returning to confront his narrow-eyed stare. 'What makes you think I need to finish school before knowing what I want? I'm not a child, Matt. I'm not.'

'Even if you sometimes act like one?' he countered, trying to make light of the situation, but she wouldn't let him.

'Do you think I'm a child?' she persisted, arching brows that were several shades darker than her hair, and he bent his head to avoid her knowing gaze.

'No,' he agreed huskily. 'No, I don't see you as a child. But that doesn't mean anything. I see what I want to see, I guess, like everyone else.'

'And—and what do you see?' she prompted, leaning towards him so that only the strength of his fingers gripping her upper arms prevented her from touching him.

Matthew lifted his head, his features taut with the control he was putting on himself. 'I see—temptation,' he muttered, expelling his breath on a heavy sigh. 'Rachel, let's go out somewhere and discuss this. I'll take you for a drive, if you like. We could even go over to Windermere and have dinner. You won't be wanting burnt toast——'

'Why can't we stay here?'

Rachel's softly spoken words stopped him dead for a moment, but then, as if tormented beyond measure by her irresponsibility, he let her go and turned abruptly away. 'You know why,' he grated, striding angrily towards the door. 'I'll call you tomorrow. Perhaps then we can have a serious conversation.'

'Oh—wait!' Impulsively, Rachel went after him, catching him before he had a chance to open the door and sliding her arms around his waist from behind. 'Matt! *Darling!*' she breathed, against the warm hollow of his spine. Her breath moistened the fine material of his shirt, and the scent of his skin was intoxicating. 'Don't go. *Please*, don't go. I'm sorry if I've made you angry, but you don't know how you make me feel.'

'Don't I?' Matthew stood stiffly within her embrace. 'I shouldn't bank on that, if I were you.'

'What do you mean?' Rachel's hands curled over the buckle of his belt, and she felt the shudder that swept through his body.

'I mean—oh, God help me!' He twisted round to face her, and jerked her roughly into his arms. 'I mean, I've been trying to fight what *you* make *me* feel!' he groaned harshly. 'But a man can only stand so much, and you are driving me *insane!*'

'Matt——' she began unsteadily, shivering at the sexual urgency of his words, but he didn't let her go. His hand at her nape tipped her face up to his, and his mouth came down on hers with a driving urgency.

Rachel's senses swam at the first touch of his lips on hers. The undisguised hunger of his caress sent the blood rushing thickly through her veins, and no experience she

had had thus far had prepared her for the eager response
of her own body. Until that moment she had been unaware of the possibility of losing her head, but as
Matthew's hands slid down her back, moulding her
yielding softness to his hard, muscled frame, she was
completely incapable of offering any resistance.

Not that she really wanted to. Any latent sense of re-
straint was totally eclipsed by the unfamiliar needs raging
inside her. The weeks of being with Matthew, of being
tantalised by his dark good looks and lazy charm, had
stirred her senses, and the accumulation of their mutual
desires was now blazing out of control.

'Oh, Matt...' she breathed, when he released her
mouth to seek the palpitating pulse below her jawline,
and he made a strangled sound of protest.

'Don't—don't ask me to stop,' he told her unevenly,
and she made a little negative movement of her head.

'I—I wasn't going to,' she whispered against his neck,
and with a shudder his mouth sought hers again.

The entry of his tongue was an intimate invasion, and
her knees turned to jelly beneath her. Plunging into her
mouth, it took her breath away, and she clung to him
helplessly as he plundered her sweetness.

'I did warn you,' he said against her ear, his arms the
only support she had, and she burrowed instinctively
against him.

'I'm not complaining, am I?' she got out jerkily, and
with a sound of desperation he pulled her down on to
the sofa.

With his mouth still silencing any protest she might
have made, his hand slid beneath the loose T-shirt, and
presently she felt his fingers fumbling with the fastening
of her bra.

'Wait,' she said, lifting a trembling hand to loosen the
clip between her breasts, and he sighed in satisfaction
as his hand closed over one small mound.

'You're beautiful,' he groaned, burying his face between her breasts, and she shuddered uncontrollably. 'So
beautiful,' he added, his thumb enticing one sensitised

nipple to peak against his palm. 'And—I want you, here—and now.'

'I want you, too,' she told him unsteadily, and, even though she wasn't entirely sure what that admission actually meant, she knew she couldn't let him go.

'Oh, Rachel,' he muttered, climbing over her and cupping her flushed face between his palms. 'We shouldn't be doing this; you know that, don't you?'

'I know it's what I want,' she replied, intensely conscious of his straddled form, of the rough texture of the couch pillows at her back, and of Matthew's arousal, an unmistakable swelling against his tight jeans, only inches from her face...

'God!' he groaned, and with a tense deliberation he tugged the T-shirt up and over her head. The bra was easily disposed of, and then, as she lay beneath him, naked and exposed from the waist up, and achingly vulnerable, 'Am I a complete bastard?'

'I don't think so,' she breathed huskily. 'Oh, Matt— kiss me! *Please*...'

And he did. But his shirt buttons were digging into her breasts, and when she protested he brought her hands to the fastenings. 'You do it,' he said against her mouth, and with trembling fingers she loosened the shirt and then eased it off his shoulders, until he could shrug out of it. Then he came down to her again, and now the light covering of fine dark hair on his chest was a tantalising abrasion.

But it wasn't enough. Even in her innocence, she knew she wouldn't be satisfied until there were no clothes between them. She wanted to feel Matthew's legs against hers, his flanks, his thighs, the flat planes of his stomach—and his sex, that most of all.

Almost instinctively her hands sought the buckle of his belt, and he levered himself up on to his knees to make it easier for her. At the same time he unfastened the button at her waist and pressed the zip down to its fullest extent. His eyes narrowed when he saw the bikini briefs beneath, and he ran one finger from the low waistband down over the quivering core of her womanhood.

She shuddered then, her hands going automatically to stop him, and, aware of her inexperience, he unzipped his own trousers and pushed them down to his knees. Now only the thin silk of his briefs contained his maleness, and Rachel couldn't look at him any more.

'Relax,' he breathed, bending towards her, and she jerked uncontrollably when he took one taut nipple between his lips.

Immediately a knife-sharp wave of heat swept over her, and she shook helplessly beneath his hands. Dear God, what was he doing? She choked, opening her eyes. But the sight of him suckling at her breast sent another shaft of heat prickling down into her stomach, and from there to the moist place between her legs. The darkness of his head against her breast was a shattering image, and almost involuntarily her hands came up to cradle his head.

Meanwhile, she felt him easing her jeans and panties down her legs, and presently he shifted to remove his own pants. And now she could feel the burning length of him against her thigh, and his leg slid between hers, his knee nudging the quivering juncture of her legs.

'Good?' he murmured, his lips drifting down over her midriff to her navel, and when she felt his tongue laving her stomach she was unable to do anything more than nod. But when he would have parted her legs she uttered a choked protest, and with a regretful sigh he returned to her mouth. 'One thing at a time,' he reassured her gently, and then, with his tongue silencing the cry that flew to her lips, he eased himself into her. 'It's all right,' he whispered against her lips, as a latent sense of panic caused her to resist him at last. 'I love you,' he added, licking the treacherous tears from her cheek. 'And when people love one another, it's the most beautiful thing in the world.'

CHAPTER EIGHT

AND it had been. Even though she had been half afraid she was going to make a fool of herself, that evening Rachel had discovered the true extent of her own sexuality. Of course, she acknowledged unwillingly now, Matthew had been a good teacher. Some might say an expert teacher, she appended bitterly. But, for whatever reason, he had been gentle with her, and although she had been totally inexperienced he had made it good for her.

Which was no mean feat, considering her initial reaction to his lovemaking, she conceded. For all she had wanted him so badly, the realisation had been not a little frightening. The feel of his powerful body lying dormant inside her had filled her with alarm, and, although at that moment she had had no real conception of what was involved, she had been half regretting her impulsiveness.

But Matthew had known how she was feeling, and instead of ravaging her, which he had confessed afterwards he had wanted to do, he had slowly restored her confidence. Allowing the palpitating nerves that surrounded him to subside, he let his mouth induce the same urgent needs she had been experiencing before he'd thrust himself upon her. Stroking and nuzzling her breasts, laving the nipples with his tongue, and sometimes taking the whole areola into his mouth, he gradually brought her to a trembling state of expectancy, and only then did he begin to move inside her.

She had thought it would be painful, but it wasn't. Her body was more than ready for his, and as he found his rhythm her muscles tightened convulsively around him. 'Oh, God,' she heard him whisper, as her hands

clutched his broad shoulders, her nails digging into his
damp skin. 'God, Rachel, you are beautiful! Don't fight
it, sweetheart. Come on—let it go...'

The memory of that moment, when their two bodies had
simultaneously splintered into sexual fulfilment, still had
the power to stir her, and Rachel moved restlessly between the silken sheets. No other man had ever even
tempted her to test that perfection, and, although she
had had friends, she had had no other lovers.

Naturally, their marriage had been the talk of the
village, and the surrounding area. That Matthew Conroy,
the eligible heir to the Conroy estate, should choose to
take an eighteen-year-old receptionist as his wife had been
little short of a scandal, and among the greatest per-
petrators of the story had been Rachel's aunt herself.

But, in spite of everything, they had got married, and
they had been happy—for a while at least. To begin with,
Matthew had been very understanding about her final
examinations, and her desire to continue with her job
at Kirkstone Television. Her initial spell of helping out
with the production of *Newsreel* had been extended when
Lynn Turner had left to have her baby, and her aptitude
had been such that Simon Motley had offered her a full-
time job as an assistant researcher.

Of course, they had had problems, as all newly married
couples did. The fact that Matthew's mother still lived
at Rothmere had been a continual bone of contention,
and Lady Olivia had lost no opportunity to criticise her
daughter-in-law.

But, on the whole, they had ridden all the difficulties,
their continuing delight in each other more than making
up for other people's interference.

And it was this aspect of their relationship which had
kept them together as long as they had been, Rachel reflected grimly. They had been so good together, and any
problems they'd had had been quickly erased by the
frantic heat of their lovemaking. They hadn't seemed
able to get enough of one another, she remembered now.

It hadn't even been unusual for Matthew to come to the television station at lunchtime, and lock both of them in the station director's office. So it was appropriate that when the break came it should involve the very substance of their feelings for one another. How could she ever forget the horror she had felt on discovering Matthew had been unfaithful to her? And with her own cousin, her own flesh and blood.

Of course, she had always known that Barbara had been jealous of her. After her marriage, her relationship with her erstwhile family had not improved, and visiting the vicarage had always been a traumatic occasion. Naturally, Matthew had usually accompanied her and, because her uncle had appreciated the gesture, she had never suggested otherwise. But it had been hard to ignore the way Barbara had behaved with her husband, aided and abetted by Aunt Maggie, whose resentment had coloured every word she spoke. But for Rachel, watching her cousin smile and flutter her eyelashes every time Matthew said anything even remotely amusing, it had been a nail-biting experience. And, although he had sometimes teased her that she was jealous, too, the maliciousness of Barbara's actions had inspired a nameless dread.

They had been married over two years, and Rachel had just been offered the chance to work in front of the cameras, when Matthew had decided it was time they started a family. The idea had come, Rachel knew, from a conversation Aunt Maggie had instigated on their last visit to the vicarage. Although her aunt could have had no desire for them to cement their relationship with the advent of a child, her comments had been unquestionably provocative. She had known, as well as everyone else, that Rachel was just beginning to make her mark at Kirkstone Television. Matthew had always been generous in his praise of his wife's accomplishments, and he had made no secret of the fact that she had been offered the chance to co-present the evening's features programme. However, even he had not been immune from sly aspersions cast on his masculinity, and Aunt Maggie's casual suggestion that perhaps Rachel's job was in compensation for not having children had been sufficiently barbed to stir his sensitivities.

And, even though he had to acknowledge that her aunt's remarks had been deliberately cruel, the notion behind them took root. So much so that they had their first really serious row over Rachel's refusal to even consider having a child, and when he flushed her contraceptive pills down the toilet she spent several nights in another room.

That particular argument blew over, of course, but it was not the last. The more popular Rachel became at the television studios, the more determined Matthew seemed to make her give it all up. Even though he knew she hadn't started taking the birth-control pill again after their reconciliation, he still persisted in goading her, and, although she discovered later that Aunt Maggie had been fuelling the fires of his anger, she couldn't have succeeded without his consent.

And, in all honesty, Rachel was not opposed to the idea of having a baby. What she was opposed to was Matthew's arrogant assumption that he could rule her life. Nevertheless, as month succeeded month and she didn't conceive, she had to face the possibility that perhaps she couldn't.

It was a traumatic time, she remembered unwillingly, and even her success as a television presenter couldn't possibly assuage her unhappiness. She went from being determined not to have a baby to wanting one desperately, and all without Matthew's sympathy, or knowledge.

It was then that Barbara started coming to the house to help Matthew. As a director of several other companies as well as Kirkstone Television, he was a busy man, and once again it had been Aunt Maggie's suggestion that Barbara should help out as part-time secretary. She had nothing else to do, having still not found a job, and Aunt Maggie said he would be doing her a service by giving her some real work experience. Of course, Matthew had Patrick Malloy to do most of his secretarial work, but there was no denying that another typist would be useful. In consequence, Rachel came home from work many evenings to find her husband and her cousin sharing an after-work drink in the library, and even though Lady Olivia didn't approve of the situation either there was nothing they could do.

For her part, Rachel's hands were tied. She could hardly ask Matthew to dismiss her cousin when there was nothing she could do to take her place. And she could hardly tell him she wanted a baby when it was becoming distressingly obvious that she couldn't have one. For, in spite of their increasing polarisation in daylight hours, at night her husband still came to her bed as regularly as ever. That aspect of their relationship was as satisfactory as it had ever been—although there were times, she knew, when Matthew despised himself for his need of her.

And then, one evening, she was late arriving home. Very late, she recalled bitterly, wondering if even then she could have saved her marriage. But by the time she arrived home, it was too late. The damage had been done. And nothing Matthew could say or do could persuade her to forgive him.

She used to drive herself home in those days, Matthew having taught her to drive soon after their marriage. He had even bought her a car—a sporty little Peugeot—to enable her to get about when he was unable to escort her.

She remembered that on the way home she had been thinking that perhaps tonight she might conceive. Lady Olivia was away, for once—a too infrequent occurrence—and she was anticipating them having the place to themselves with a genuine sense of excitement. The doctors she had consulted had all been of the opinion that she was trying too hard to have this baby, but they didn't understand what it meant to her. They didn't know she was in danger of losing the only man she would ever love. Maybe tonight she would succeed, she told herself eagerly. If she didn't, it wouldn't be her fault.

It was after ten when she parked the car at the side of the house and entered the building. The sight of her uncle's car parked on the drive was daunting—it meant Barbara was still here—but she determined not to let that faze her. Entering the house, she went straight to the library, prepared to apologise herself, if necessary, for the delay in getting home. But there was no one there. Empty glasses stood on the cabinet, and an empty bottle of Scotch was rolled significantly under a chair, but the room itself was empty.

Her first thoughts, she remembered, were that they must have gone out, and although that idea wasn't appealing she could only blame herself. After all, she was invariably home by seven-thirty, and just because there had been an electrical failure at the studios, there was no reason why she shouldn't have phoned. But the situation between her and Matthew was so volatile at the moment that she had found excuses not to fuel his impatience, and it had never occurred to her that it might precipitate disaster.

Watkins was in the hall when she came out of the library, but when she asked him if he knew where Matthew was he was strangely reticent. But his eyes did turn guiltily to the ceiling above their heads, and with a growing sense of apprehension Rachel left him to run headlong up the stairs.

She had heard their voices before she reached the suite of rooms which she and Matthew shared. She remembered hearing Barbara's laughter, and Matthew's rueful chuckle, so that when she threw the door open she was half prepared for what confronted her.

But even then the reality was so much worse than the anticipation. Rachel had stared aghast at her half-naked husband, his chest bare, his trousers pooled around his ankles, and Barbara's hands hooked into the waistband of his briefs, caught in the act of pushing the black silk over his lean hips. Barbara herself was almost decent, although her unbuttoned blouse and mussed hair spoke of a greater intimacy. And, of all of them, she was the one with the least to lose, the one with the most to gain.

The tableau was imprinted on Rachel's mind for months to come. How she had stood there, looking at them, without throwing up, was an achievement in itself. How could Matthew have done it? Had their relationship sunk to such an ebb that he could actually justify his actions? For there had been no shame, no contrition. Only a bland defiance in the face of her distress.

Of course, he had been drunk, she had realised that later. Not falling-down drunk, not incoherently intoxicated, but coldly, and calculatedly, immune to any recrimination. He had simply appeared not to care what she thought of him, and Barbara had burst into crocodile tears, with more than a hint of triumph.

There was no row then. That came the following morning, after Rachel had spent a sleepless night in a spare room. She had no idea how long Barbara had stayed, or indeed if she was still in the house, when she went downstairs before breakfast. But Matthew was waiting in the library for her, and the exchange that followed was just as horrible as she had anticipated.

What could she expect, he demanded, when it was obvious she thought more about her bloody job than him? Why should she complain if he found sympathy elsewhere? Their marriage was just a sham anyway; she had no intention of ever giving him a family.

There was more in the same vein—angry, bitter words that tore through Rachel's stand for independence, and found it wanting. She was just a shell, he told her, a miserable, useless thing, who held on to her puerile career because it was the only thing she was good at. Just because they were married there was no reason for her to think she was indispensable. If he wanted to have sex with someone else, he would do it, and to hell with her.

Rachel remembered him slamming out of the house after that, and her being scarcely able to climb the stairs again. But climb them she did, and she packed a suitcase with sufficient clothes to see her through the next couple of days before following him out of the house. She didn't take the car. She called a taxi. And only Watkins saw her go, a troubled, anxious figure.

The ironic thing was, Matthew came after her. She had never thought he would, but he did. It wasn't difficult for him to find the address of the holiday apartment she had temporarily leased in Penrith, and, once it became apparent that she wasn't coming back, he came to find her.

But it was too late. She refused to speak to him, locking herself behind closed doors and not answering his phone calls. Of course, it couldn't go on. Her work at the studios was suffering, and she knew that it was only a matter of time before she would be forced to leave the area.

Her uncle came to see her, too, but he had little more success. His assertion that Barbara was grief-stricken by what had happened was not quite believable, particularly when Barbara herself showed so little remorse. And when Aunt Maggie came to see her six weeks later to impart the news that Barbara was expecting a baby, Rachel didn't hesitate before seeking a divorce.

The days and weeks that followed were the worst kind of purgatory. But at least Matthew no longer pestered her. Evidently Barbara's news, combined with the divorce papers he had been served, had at last killed any lingering responsibility he felt towards her. And when Simon Motley offered to use his influence to find her a job in London Rachel jumped at the chance to leave this miserable period of her life behind.

But it was not quite over. A week after moving into the apartment that the London studios had found for her in Kensington, Rachel was taken ill in the night. Racked with pain, she could do nothing until morning, when she rang the studios and explained that she thought she ought to see a doctor. She was bleeding, and although

she thought it might be her period she had never been
so sick before.

The doctor was sympathetic, but unable to help her.
It was too late. She was having a miscarriage, he told
her gently. But, because she had waited so long before
calling him, there was nothing he could do...

Of course, she had been shattered at the news, particularly so after everything that had gone before. For days
and days she had been unable to do anything but cry,
and, although the doctor reassured her that it was a perfectly natural reaction, she knew better.

It was just something else to blame herself for, and it
took months, *years*, before she was able to get it into
perspective. She knew it had been walking in on Barbara
and her husband that had put all other considerations
out of her head, but for a long while she continued to
bear the burden for her baby's loss of life. It had been
a little boy, they had told her, when she had asked,
perfect in every way. Matthew's son. Perhaps the only
thing that could have saved their marriage, and she
hadn't even known.

That was when Justin had been such a comfort.
Although their association had been brief up to that
point, he had made her feel she had at least one friend
in London. But it had been a while before she'd told
him the full story, in all its ugly detail.

CHAPTER NINE

RACHEL was out of bed and sitting by the window when there was a scuffled sound outside her door the next morning. She was feeling much better: not half as shaky as she had felt the previous day. But she was unwillingly coming to accept Dr Newman's opinion that it would be days at least before she was well enough to drive back to London, and although she was impatient there was nothing she could do.

Now, hearing the curious sound of rustling paper, she got up from her chair and walked, albeit a little unsteadily, across to the door and pulled it open.

Rosemary practically tumbled into the room. She had evidently been crouching down, probably looking through the keyhole, Rachel thought resignedly, and when she'd opened the door the little girl had lost her balance.

'We must stop meeting like this,' she remarked drily, as the child picked herself up off the floor and stuffed the bag of sweets she was holding into her jeans pocket. 'Did you want something?'

Rosemary's cheeks were pink, and for once she looked almost attractive. It was mostly her sallow complexion that gave her face such an unhealthy appearance, but now, with colour in her cheeks and her hair neatly combed into a tight braid, she appeared quite pretty.

'I came to see how you were,' she answered now, as Rachel made her way back to her chair. Rosemary watched her sink rather weakly on to the cushions, and then gave a rueful grimace. 'I s'pose it was my fault again that you cut your head on the rocks. I came to say I'm sorry. I'm sorry you got hurt.'

'Yes. So am I,' murmured Rachel, leaning her head back against the pillows behind her, and feeling ridiculously weary after her brief exertion. 'But don't worry, it wasn't your fault. Not really. I just—stumbled, that's all. It could have happened to anyone.'

Rosemary hesitated a moment, biting her lip, and then she turned and closed the door. 'Daddy was ever so worried about you,' she confided, leaving the door to approach the woman. 'I think he thought he had *killed* you,' she added dramatically. 'You were just lying there on the sand, not moving. And then I saw the blood, and he just flaked!'

'Flaked?' echoed Rachel wearily, half wishing the child would go so that she could close her eyes. But, having come to a dubious understanding with the little girl, she had no desire to resurrect her hostility. All Rosemary really needed was attention, and she wondered how long it was since either of her parents had given her any.

'You know,' Rosemary was saying now. 'He kind of— went all to pieces. Grandmama says it was because of the shock, but I think it was something else.'

'Do you?' Rachel sighed and met the little girl's gaze with wary eyes. There were times when Rosemary could be unnervingly perceptive, and she was half afraid of what she was about to reveal.

'Yes.' Rosemary paused, pulling the bag of sweets out of her pocket again, and offering one to Rachel. When she refused, Rosemary took a toffee for herself, and unwrapped it with the air of someone about to impart a state secret. 'I think my father was so upset because he likes you——'

'*Likes* me?'

'Yes. Oh, I know he seemed angry——'

'He didn't *seem* angry, Rosemary, he *was* angry,' Rachel informed her flatly. And then, after a moment, 'Mostly because you hadn't told anyone where you were going.'

'Oh, *that*!'

Rosemary was disparaging, but Rachel lifted her head. 'Yes, that,' she agreed, regarding the little girl reprovingly. 'You know that was naughty, don't you?'

'Well, no one's cared where I was before,' retorted the child, scuffing her shoe against the carpet. ' 'Cept Grandmama, sometimes.'

'Oh, Rosemary, that's not true!'

'It *is* true.' The little girl was adamant. 'Ask anyone. Mrs Moffat says I'm just allowed to run wild.'

And that was so adult a statement that Rachel had to believe she had heard it. Trying to ignore her own feelings, she said consolingly, 'Mrs Moffat was probably talking about—well, while your mother was ill. Obviously, she couldn't look after you then, and your father was very upset——'

'No.'

Rosemary pushed her hands into her pockets, and looked down at her feet, and Rachel sighed. 'No, what?' she prompted gently. 'No, Mummy couldn't look after you——?'

'No, she never looked after me,' mumbled Rosemary bitterly. 'She was always too busy to talk to me, and Daddy is never here.'

Rachel gasped. 'I'm sure you're wrong. About your mummy not caring about you, I mean. And—and your father is a busy man.'

Rosemary looked unconvinced. 'Anyway, Miss Seton took care of me,' she said. 'Until Daddy got rid of her and hired Agnetha.'

'Miss Seton?'

'She was nice.' The child's face relaxed, transforming her pale features. The resemblance to Matthew had never been more marked, and Rachel's stomach muscles tightened. 'I wanted her to stay, but Daddy said she was too old, and that I was too old to need a nursemaid.'

'I see.' The identity of Miss Seton resolved, Rachel breathed a little more easily.

'Anyway, I don't need anyone to look after me,' Rosemary asserted suddenly. 'I can look after myself.

Better than you can, it seems to me. Why didn't you tell Daddy why you were chasing me?'

'Oh . . .' That was not so easy to answer, and Rachel lay back against her pillows rather tiredly. 'Let's say it's our secret,' she murmured. Then, 'Does he know you buy cigarettes at the village shop?'

'No.' Rosemary hunched her shoulders. 'But he knows about the cigarettes. Agnetha told him.'

'Agnetha?'

Rosemary nodded. 'She found them in my bedroom and split on me,' she answered sulkily. 'Daddy was furious. He says he's going to send me away to school because I'm so disobedient. I bet he used to smoke when he was my age. And I bet Grandpa didn't punish him!'

'I wouldn't be too sure about that, if I were you,' Rachel was saying rather drily when the bedroom door abruptly opened to admit the small yet imposing figure of Lady Olivia.

Rachel offered an inward groan at this unwelcome intrusion, and Rosemary adopted a defiant stance, as if this was the last place she was supposed to be. It probably was, acknowledged Rachel wearily. Matthew did not approve of her associating with his daughter, and she didn't suppose his mother did either.

'So this is where you are, Rosemary,' her grandmother observed now, her sharp eyes briefly shifting to Rachel's drawn features before returning to the child. 'I thought your father warned you about disobeying him again. Run along, at once. Agnetha is waiting. And no slipping out to the stables. Mr Ryan has orders not to let you near Marigold for at least a week.'

'Yes, Grandmama.'

Rosemary had little alternative but to submit, and, looking at Lady Olivia's grim features, Rachel couldn't help thinking she would have done the same. She hoped the old lady hadn't come here to cause trouble. Just at this moment, she didn't have the strength to defend herself.

Offering the child a rueful smile as she let herself out of the door, Rachel made a determined effort to gather her resources. She and Lady Olivia had had many confrontations in the past, but never had she felt less equipped to deal with another. The old lady mustn't guess that, though. She already possessed an overwhelming advantage.

'Well, Rachel,' she said now, as the door closed behind Rosemary. Slim and elegant in her simple but expensive grey dress, her almost white hair coiled into a knot on top of her head, Matthew's mother seated herself on the ottoman, crossing her ankles in true aristocratic fashion. 'Dr Newman tells me you're feeling a little better this morning.'

'Yes, I am.' Rachel's fingers curled defensively over her wrist. 'I'm sorry I'm being such a nuisance.'

'Hardly that.' Lady Olivia's inbred sense of courtesy did not allow for rudeness. And it would have been rude to imply that Rachel had chosen to be brought here. After all, she had been unconscious when Matthew had carried her into the house. 'However, you must admit this is an unusual situation.'

'Yes.' Rachel took a steadying breath. 'Well, you can be sure that as soon as I'm able to leave, I will.'

Lady Olivia made no answer to this, merely linked her somewhat gnarled hands together in her lap and allowed a pregnant silence. Then, apparently having some trouble marshalling her words, she remarked unexpectedly, 'You appear to have made a hit with Rosemary.'

'I wouldn't say that.' Rachel swallowed.

'I would.' Lady Olivia's eyes, so like Matthew's, speared her with a raking glance. 'She's not usually friendly with strangers.'

'No.' Rachel wondered how she was supposed to respond to that. 'Well, I suppose we have a lot in common.'

'You think so?' Lady Olivia frowned. 'I don't see the connection.'

No, you wouldn't, thought Rachel tersely, quelling the urge to involve herself in Rosemary's affairs. 'My mother died when I was very young, too,' she compromised.

'Ah, yes.' The old lady inclined her head. 'But your circumstances were slightly different. And Barbara had been ill for quite some time.'

Now it was Rachel's turn to accept her words without answering. She was half afraid she might say something she would regret, and Matthew's mother was a past mistress at inducing the unwary comment.

'So—what were you and Rosemary talking about?' she asked at last, when it became evident that Rachel was not about to enlighten her uninvited. 'Forgive me, but I couldn't help overhearing you say that you wouldn't be too sure about something. What was that? Was she asking your advice?'

Rachel was tempted to tell her to mind her own business, but she didn't. All the same, only Matthew's mother would have dared to ask such a question, and Rachel could feel her hackles rising with well-remembered indignation. Only the suspicion that any prevarication on her part might bring some further punishment down on Rosemary's head forced her to bite her tongue.

'She's—concerned that her father may decide to send her away to boarding-school,' she replied, after a moment, and Lady Olivia frowned.

'But you don't think he will?' she queried tersely, and Rachel realised why she should interpret her remarks in that way.

'I really don't know what Matt's intentions are towards her,' she responded carefully. 'But I think he should be careful. She seems a very distrustful child.'

Lady Olivia sat up straighter. 'You think so, do you?'

Rachel's hesitation was barely perceptible. 'Yes.'

'And what would you know about it?' enquired the old lady sharply, and Rachel realised she had gone that little bit too far in expressing her opinion. 'It's not as if you know anything about children,' she added, her lined

features taut with indignation. 'Are you suggesting I
should trust your assessment of Rosemary's needs above
that of my son?'

'No. No, of course not.' Rachel sighed now. 'It's just
that—well, I got the impression that she feels——' She
broke off at that point. She had been going to say
'neglected', but after Lady Olivia's reaction to her earlier
words she stifled the criticism. Once again, she was
compelled to remind herself that Rosemary's problems
had nothing to do with her. Just because she felt some
sympathy for the child, there was no reason to provoke
Matthew's mother's antagonism towards herself.

'I hardly see how peddling claptrap to the masses
equips you in child psychology,' the old lady declared
bluntly. 'Why is it that women who consider child-
bearing an outdated vocation nevertheless feel themselves capable of deciding what's best for other people's
offspring?'

'I never said that.'

'But you do have doubts about the suitability of
Rosemary's upbringing!'

'I—suspect—she may have had a raw deal, yes.' Rachel
couldn't prevent the involuntary admission.

'A raw deal?' Lady Olivia's lip curled. 'But not half
such a raw deal as you dealt her father, hmm? How dare
you impugn his intentions when your own behaviour
leaves so much to be desired?'

Rachel offered an inward groan. Getting into this kind
of a confrontation with Matthew's mother had been
something she had hoped to avoid. And in her present
state of uncertainty she was definitely not equipped to
deal with it.

'Forget what I said,' she murmured, wishing Nurse
Douglas would appear to rescue her. 'As you say, it's
nothing to do with me. How Matt chooses to educate
his daughter is obviously not my concern.'

'No, it's not.' But Lady Olivia was not prepared to
leave it there. Rachel suspected she had played right into
the old lady's hands by offering an opinion, and re-

sentiments long since buried were rearing their ugly heads. 'It's ironic, don't you think, that the woman who refused to have my son's child should now be offering him advice?'

'I didn't——' The unwary words were almost spoken, and Rachel felt the hot colour rise into her cheeks.

'You didn't—what?' Matthew's mother was quick to note her heightened colour. 'You didn't offer him advice?' She paused. 'Or you didn't refuse to give him a child?' Her lips twisted. 'Oh, come now, Rachel, you can't expect anyone to believe that!'

'I don't care what you believe.' Rachel closed her eyes. 'Would you ask Nurse Douglas to come in, please? I'd like to get back into bed.'

Her aunt and uncle came to see her during the afternoon. By then, Rachel had had another nap and was feeling more ready to face a second wave of criticism. But in the event Matthew accompanied his in-laws into the room, and, evidently much to Aunt Maggie's chagrin, he stayed.

In consequence, the conversation was much less vindictive than it might have been. Even so, her aunt couldn't resist voicing a little of her resentment that Rachel should be usurping Matthew's hospitality.

'You have a perfectly good room at the vicarage, Rachel,' she declared, with barely suppressed irritation. 'There is no earthly need for you to impose yourself on—on—well, on the Conroys.'

'Ah, yes, but I wouldn't dream of putting you to such trouble,' Matthew essayed, before Rachel could answer. 'I know how much your husband depends upon you, and it wouldn't be fair to expect you to care for an invalid on top of everything else.'

'I—well...' Aunt Maggie was apparently lost for words. 'That may be so, but——'

'Matt does have a point, dear,' Geoffrey Barnes intoned, drawing a distinctly malevolent glare from his wife which, fortunately, only Rachel intercepted. 'It's very kind of you, Matt. Very kind indeed. Maggie does too much; I'm always telling her that.'

'Geoff——'

'I hope I won't have to impose on anybody for much longer,' Rachel interposed quickly, feeling uncomfortably like the skeleton at the feast. 'Perhaps another couple of days——'

'We'll let the doctor decide that,' declared Matthew, his words successfully circumventing any alternative suggestion, and Rachel wondered why he was taking it upon himself to defend her. For he must know, as well as anyone, how her aunt must be feeling.

'I think that's the most sensible course,' her uncle approved, seemingly unaware of his wife's indignation. 'It's reassuring to know you're in good hands, my dear.'

'And you don't think the fact that Barbara has just died makes the situation just the the tiniest bit questionable?' persisted Aunt Maggie tensely. 'I mean—everyone knows who Rachel is—*was*!'

'Aunt Maggie——'

'I don't believe what anyone else thinks is of any consequence,' responded Matthew smoothly. 'And now, I think, we should allow Rachel to rest. That is what the doctor recommends, and I know you are as anxious as I am to see her restored to full health.'

It was tactically unassailable, and Rachel guessed that her aunt was wishing she had chosen some other method of making her point. But, in the circumstances, she was obliged to concede defeat, and Rachel breathed a sigh of relief as the door closed behind them. So much anger, so much bitterness, she thought wearily. Did no one feel any sympathy for her? After all, she wasn't the one who had been unfaithful.

She had insisted on getting up again to receive her visitors, but now she looked reluctantly towards the bed. Strong emotions were such a drain on her resources, and not one of her callers seemed to care about the fact. Even Rosemary had been an innocent source of turmoil. Why had she had to tell her that her father had been concerned about her, for heaven's sake? What could he possibly have said to make the little girl think he liked her? It was all too obscure and unbelievable, after the way he had behaved at the funeral. And she was too tired to make any sense of it anyway.

CHAPTER TEN

RACHEL felt strong enough to put her clothes on the next day. It was amazing how much better she felt after a decent night's sleep, and her anxieties of the previous day seemed less of a problem this morning.

Dr Newman made his regular call as she was finishing her breakfast, sitting at the small table in the window embrasure, overlooking the lawned garden and the lake beyond. After examining her head, he pronounced himself satisfied with the progress she was making.

'The cut is healing nicely,' he said, accepting her offer of a cup of coffee, and seating himself opposite her at the linen-covered table. 'And you are definitely looking brighter. If this goes on, I may consider revising my estimate of two weeks, and say you might be able to return to work in ten days.'

'Ten days?' Rachel shook her head, remembering she had still to get in touch with Justin. She was not looking forward to making that phone call. After the way he had reacted when she'd asked for these four days, she had no illusions but that he would be furious, particularly when he found out where she was staying. Forcing a smile, she asked lightly, 'Is that your best offer?'

'I'm afraid so. And it's only a provisional prognosis.' The doctor regarded her curiously. 'You're very anxious to leave here, aren't you?'

Rachel looked down into the cup of coffee she was holding to avoid his shrewd gaze. 'I do have a job to do,' she reminded him evenly. 'And I presume you'll have no objections if I return to London in a couple of days.'

'If all goes well.' Dr Newman was evidently not prepared to make any reckless pronouncements. 'Shall we

say I'll consider the possibility towards the end of the
week? Until then, I'm afraid, you'll have to accept your
host's hospitality.'

'But you don't think there will be any complications?'
she ventured.

'No.' The doctor inclined his head agreeably. 'But that
doesn't mean there won't be any, so don't build your
hopes too high. However, you can go outside, if you feel
up to it. As long as you wrap up warmly, and don't do
anything too energetic.'

Rachel gave him a guarded look. 'All right.'

'Good.' He finished his coffee and rose smoothly to
his feet. 'And now, I'm afraid I must take my leave of
you. Regrettably, Sundays are much like any other day
in my profession.'

Rachel nodded. 'Thank you for coming.'

'It was my pleasure.' He gave her a rueful smile as he
walked towards the door. 'Not all my patients are half
so agreeable, believe me.'

His compliment compensated a little for the disappointment she had felt when he'd refused to be more
specific about her leaving, and she was still considering
what he had said when Nurse Douglas reappeared. She
had left the room while Dr Newman had coffee with his
patient, but now she came back to remove the breakfast
dishes.

'By the way,' she said, tutting at the fact that Rachel
had only eaten one slice of toast, 'Mr Conroy wants to
see you. Shall I send him in?'

Rachel caught her breath. 'He's outside?'

'Not precisely, no.' Nurse Douglas looked a little dis-
concerted. 'He—I—we were talking downstairs, while
you were with Dr Newman. Shall I ask him to come
up?'

'Why not?' Rachel was surprised he had asked. Or
perhaps it had just been an excuse to talk to Nurse
Douglas, she reflected, bitter that she should even care.
And, judging by the young nurse's attitude towards him,
no real excuse was needed.

He came into the room, bringing a distinct smell of outdoors with him. In tight-fitting moleskin trousers, which were in turn pushed into knee-length boots, and a black leather jacket, he had evidently been riding, and she envied him his ability to appear indifferent to his responsibilities.

However, he seemed surprised to see that she was dressed, and she was ridiculously pleased that she had chosen to put on jeans and a loose cream thigh-length sweater. She had put the casual clothes into her case at the last minute, she remembered, and she wondered if she had had some premonition that she might need them. After all, she had not intended to spend more than one night at Rothside, whereas...

'You're looking much better,' he observed, after a pregnant pause, and she wondered if he was anticipating her departure as much as she was. 'How do you feel?'

'Much—better,' she conceded tersely, linking her hands together in her lap to prevent the automatic urge to touch the dressing that had replaced the bandage only that morning. 'Dr Newman says I should be able to leave in a couple of days.'

Matthew's mouth thinned. 'I understood Newman to say that he was going to review your condition towards the end of the week,' he declared. 'You must have misunderstood him.'

'Or you did,' Rachel flared unsteadily, refusing to be intimidated. 'Um—Nurse Douglas said you wanted to speak to me. Was there a reason, or was that just an excuse to browbeat me?'

'Browbeat you?' Matthew stared at her disbelievingly. 'How have I browbeaten you? All I've done is ask how you're feeling. I'm sorry. I didn't realise that constituted a threat!'

Rachel sighed, feeling a little silly now, and not liking it a bit. After all, he had provided her with the best of medical care, and it wasn't his fault that she was taking so long to recover.

'Look,' she said, forcing herself to look at him, even though she would have preferred to look anywhere than into his lean, taut face, 'I know how—intolerable—this situation is——'

'Intolerable to whom?'

Rachel caught her lower lip between her teeth. 'Well—to your mother for one,' she said unwillingly. 'And—Aunt Maggie——'

'Ah, yes. Aunt Maggie.' Matthew hooked the chair that Dr Newman had occupied earlier towards him, and, swinging it round, he set it in front of her. Then, strad-dling the seat so that his knee was barely inches from hers, he regarded her with a cynical gaze. 'You know, I might have expected some thanks for diverting your aunt, instead of being accused of God knows what ulterior motives!'

Rachel shifted uncomfortably. Now that he was on eye-level terms with her, it was far more difficult to maintain a composed expression, and when she did look away from his dark face she was made overwhelmingly aware of his powerful body, taut beneath the skin-tight trousers and sweatshirt. His jacket had parted to reveal the leather belt that spanned his waist, and she could smell the heat that emanated from him, and the unfor-gettable scent of his skin...

'Anyway,' he was saying now, and she dragged her senses back from the brink of disaster, 'I didn't come to argue over Newman's diagnosis, and I knew better than to expect your gratitude for anything I might do. No. I came to tell you I've spoken to your editor in London, and he quite understands that you can't poss-ibly return to work for another two weeks——'

'You've done what?' Rachel hardly let him finish, before jumping up from her seat and staring down at him with disbelieving eyes. 'You've spoken to Justin?'

'If that's Harcourt's name, I suppose so,' conceded Matthew drily, his lips tightening at her evident indig-nation. 'Look, calm down, will you? Someone had to tell him you wouldn't be back tomorrow, and how was I to know you'd be well enough to speak to him your——'

'How dare you?' Rachel was incensed. 'How dare you speak to Justin behind my back?'

'It wasn't behind your back,' said Matthew bleakly, his fingers tightening where they rested along the back of the chair. 'That's why I'm here, isn't it? To tell you that I've spoken to him.'

'You couldn't wait, could you?' Rachel was beside herself, although why she resented his interference so much, she couldn't quite have explained. Except that she had kept her life in London totally apart from Rothmere, and all it meant to her. 'You had to get involved in something that's nothing to do with you! I would have explained to Justin exactly what had happened. I would have told him where I was staying, and when I would be back.'

Matthew's face hardened, and, getting to his feet, he thrust the chair aside. 'And don't you think I was capable of doing the same?' he demanded, his tone reminding her that he had a temper, too. 'What's the matter? Is this—Justin—the new man in your life? Are you afraid I may have blown it by telling him you were with me?'

'I'm not *with* you,' Rachel retorted, frustrated by his ability to always take the upper hand. 'At least, not through choice. And my relationship with Justin is my affair, not yours. Just stay out of my life, Matt. I don't need you any more.'

'If you ever did,' muttered Matthew harshly, his eyes glittering like grey chips of granite. 'Except as a means of getting into television, of course. I mustn't forget that, must I?'

'You—bastard!'

Rachel, who had turned away from his hard, accusing face, swung back abruptly. Her balled fists itching to wipe the sarcastic expression from his narrow features, she overlooked the fact that there was a chair between them. Her knee struck the wood painfully, knocking it aside, and, instead of launching in at him with flailing fists, she stumbled and lost her balance, so that only his presence of mind and the swift support of his hands saved her from repeating the accident which had put her in this position. Strong fingers around her wrists stopped her from tumbling to the floor, but the force of her propulsion sent her thudding against his chest.

For a moment, she was too stunned by what had happened to move. Her face was pressed against the fleecy softness of his shirt, and his raw masculinity enveloped her with a strength that was far more than just physical. Then, as his arms closed around her, she was made aware of the whole length of his taut body, his thighs muscled and powerful, his hard flanks supporting her distinctly shaky legs.

'God, I thought you were going to crack your skull again,' he muttered roughly, his head bent so that his breath stirred the hairs at the side of her neck. 'Are you all right? Hell, I didn't mean to upset you.' The warm draught was like a caress. 'You shouldn't make me so mad. All I did was make a phone call!'

Rachel was trembling, and she couldn't stop it. But it wasn't just the shock that had robbed her of her control. It was Matthew, only Matthew, she knew perversely. Being held in his arms like this was both a heaven and a hell, and, no matter how she fought it, she couldn't deny her own response.

But, as if mistaking her involuntary submission, Matthew was already propelling her away from him. Holding her at arm's length, he forced her to look at him, and Rachel closed her eyes against the penetrating fire of his.

'Rachel,' he muttered, shaking her a little as she continued to evade his searching gaze. 'For God's sake, what's the matter? Do you feel sick? Faint? What?'

'I'm—all right,' she got out at last, endeavouring to free herself from his hands. Forced to open her eyes, she looked anywhere but into his face. 'It—it was just the shock, that's all. And—and I banged my knee.'

'You did? Where?' Releasing her, he dropped down on to his haunches in front of her, and to her dismay she felt his hands peeling up the leg of her jeans to expose the purpling skin. 'Hell,' he swore grimly, his fingers unbearably gentle as they probed the quivering bones, 'why do you persist in making me feel such a brute?' He tilted his head back to look up at her, and her heart palpitated at the look of naked frustration in his eyes. 'I thought I was doing you a favour, can you believe that? Instead, I've only made you hate me even more than you already did!'

'I—don't—hate you.' She could say that with all certainty. She wished to God she did. It would have been so much less painful. 'Honestly,' she added unsteadily, bending to roll down the leg of her jeans, and in so doing bringing her face within inches of Matthew's.

Afterwards, she realised that he had recognised the danger at the same moment she did. They both straightened together, and she thought his expression mirrored her own sudden sense of anguish, though there was no trace of it in his abrupt withdrawal.

'I'd better go,' he said, and his voice was almost formally detached. He picked up the chair which had caused the trouble, and deposited it back beside the table. 'Unfortunately, I can't do anything about the phone call, but there's nothing stopping you from ringing him again and putting him straight. I'll have Nurse Douglas fetch you the cordless phone——'

'Don't bother.' Rachel broke in before he had finished what he had to say. 'I—I'll speak to him later. When—when I know when I'm leaving.'

'As you wish.' Matthew made a gesture of indifference, and walked towards the door. 'I'll leave you now. If you want anything—anything at all—just ask Nurse Douglas.'

'Thank you.'

Rachel watched him let himself out of the door, and after it had closed behind him a feeling of total devastation gripped her. In the last few minutes she had run the gamut of her emotions, and she was left with the unpleasant realisation that only the strongest of these survived. And, in her case, it wasn't the contempt she had believed she would feel when she saw her ex-husband again...

Matthew reined in his mount on the lower slopes of Rothdale Pike. Running soothing hands over Saracen's neck, he surveyed the whole length of the lake, with the roofs of Rothside like stepping-stones below him. In spite of the early hour, there were already one or two white sails dotting the wide expanse of water, with a couple of windsurfers nearer at hand, riding the gentle waves.

'I don't think Marigold's very fit, Daddy!' exclaimed Rosemary, panting a little as she dug her heels into the pony's sides to urge her up the track to join her father.

'I think she's just short of exercise,' responded Matthew drily, reaching over to grasp the pony's bridle and pull her nearer. 'And remember, it could have been several more days before she got some air. I believe you were supposed to be grounded for a week.'

'Oh, it was Grandmama who said that——'

'*I* said it, too,' amended her father warningly. 'Which reminds me, you never did tell me where you got those cigarettes. Do you want to tell me now, or is it to remain a bone of contention between us?'

'Oh, Daddy!'

Rosemary sighed, and Matthew knew a moment's contrition. He hadn't meant to sound so severe, and he half wished he hadn't brought up the subject of the cigarettes—not this morning.

The decision to take his daughter riding had been a spur-of-the-moment thing. He wasn't at all sure why he had invited her to join him, except that it had something to do with what Rachel had said that morning he had caused her accident. And he *had* been the cause of it, he thought ruefully. Whatever she said, and however much he might justify to himself what had happened, the fact remained that if he had not lost his temper and pushed her she would not have fallen and injured her head.

Still, he had to admit that since that morning he had spent an awful lot of time considering what Rachel had said. He didn't want to admit it, but it was true—he did give little of his time to his daughter. Yet, while Barbara was alive, he had seldom felt a sense of guilt about it.

Perhaps if he had been able to feel that she really *was* his daughter he would have acted differently, he reflected now. Not that he had ever voiced his doubts to anyone else. Being accused of being incapable of siring a child was not something you discussed with anyone except your wife, particularly if she was the one who was making the accusation.

He shook his head. What a ruinous mess he had made of his life, he thought bitterly. How much different things might have been if he had done as his mother had wanted and married Cecily Bishop in the first place.

And yet, he and Rachel had been happy in those early days, before her career had become more important to her than he was. No one had been able to hurt them; they had been impregnable. But then the rows had begun, and his isolation had grown; and Barbara had seemed so sympathetic...

'What are you thinking about, Daddy?'

Rosemary's anxious voice dragged him back to the present, and the realisation that he had been indulging in maudlin retrospection. What did it matter now what had been said? Barbara was dead. Rosemary *was* his daughter. And, as Rachel had pointed out, she needed him if no one else did.

'Nothing,' he said now, forcing a tight smile to his lips. 'Come on, we'll ride down to the village, and get some ice-cream.

CHAPTER ELEVEN

'So, when are you coming back?'

Justin's enquiry was pleasant enough, but Rachel sensed the controlled impatience behind the words. And why not? she asked herself unhappily. When she had come north, he had expected her to be away for only two days. Those two days had now stretched to a week, and she still could give him no real definition of when she would actually return.

'I'm sure you're managing to cope,' she ventured lightly, hoping to divert him, but Justin wasn't amused.

'Oh, we're managing to cope very well,' he replied nastily, clearing his throat. 'Perhaps you should be worrying about that. We may find we manage very well without you.'

Rachel sighed. 'It's not my fault that I'm stuck up here.'

'Well, it's certainly not mine,' retorted Justin. 'If you remember, I didn't want you to go in the first place. I knew something like this would happen. I knew Conroy would find some way to keep you there.'

'Oh, don't be ridiculous!' Rachel was impatient now. 'Matt isn't responsible for what happened. That is—well, he is, I suppose. If you want to be literal about it. But it was an accident! He didn't engineer it. Heavens, I could have fallen without anyone else being involved.'

'But Conroy was involved, wasn't he? However indirectly. And I have to tell you, I don't like his attitude. Were you too scared to ring and tell me what had happened? I'm telling you, he got a great deal of enjoyment out of giving me the news.'

'Oh, Justin.' Rachel's fingers tightened around the receiver. 'You know you're exaggerating. Matt only rang

131

because he thought I wasn't up to it.' And when had she come to that conclusion? 'I intended phoning you myself. He beat me to it, that's all.'

'And have you stopped to ask yourself why?'

'I've told you why.' Rachel hated Justin in this mood. He could be so objectionable. She had seen him reduce some of the younger reporters and secretaries to tears at times, but it was a new experience for him to turn his bile on her. 'Anyway, I'm ringing you now, aren't I? What more can I do? You know I'll be back as quickly as I can.'

'Do I?' He didn't sound convinced. 'You still haven't told me when that's likely to be.'

'Because I don't know!' exclaimed Rachel in exasperation. 'But—well, I went outdoors yesterday for the first time, and the doctor thinks that in another week——'

Justin snorted. 'Another week?'

'That I should be well enough to drive back to town, at least.'

'But not to work?' The sarcasm was back, and Rachel shook her head.

'Not—immediately, perhaps. But in a couple of days——'

'So we can't expect you back in the office for at least another two weeks?'

'Well,' Rachel licked her dry lips, 'it's Tuesday today. Perhaps a week on Thursday, hmm?'

'What choice do I have?'

Justin sounded furious, and justifiably so, thought Rachel unwillingly. But there was no point in prevaricating. Unless she was prepared to override Dr Newman's advice and make her own arrangements, she was compelled to remain where she was.

'I'm sorry,' she murmured now, and she heard his angry intake of breath.

'So am I,' he conceded, without any sigh of compassion, and before she could say anything more he had slammed down his receiver.

Rachel was sliding the small aerial belonging to the cordless phone back into its socket when someone knocked at her door. Putting the phone down, she rose to her feet as the door was propelled inward, and then sank back into her seat when Rosemary's head appeared. 'Can I come in?'

'Can I stop you?' Rachel pushed the anxieties caused by her call to Justin aside, and smiled at the little girl. 'What do you want?' she asked, glancing towards the windows, where she could see the sun gleaming on the lake. 'Isn't it too nice a day to be indoors?'

'Not 'cording to Grandmama,' replied Rosemary, with a grimace, and Rachel frowned.

'Oh, but I thought—that is—Mrs Moffat said that your father took you riding the other morning.'

'Yes, he did. Yesterday,' Rosemary nodded. 'But—well, anyway, today he's gone off to Carlisle, and Grandmama says I have to do some reading.'

'Reading?' Rachel ran her tongue over her lower lip. 'But you do go to school, don't you?'

'In Rothside,' agreed Rosemary quickly. But then, with a grimace, she added, 'I don't know if I'll be going back, though. Daddy was awfully cross. And just when he was being nice, too.'

Rachel shook her head. 'Matt—I mean, your daddy was cross about you going to school?' She was confused.

'No!' Rosemary hunched her small shoulders. 'About the cigarettes. He found out, you see. Mrs Reed told him.'

'She did?' Rachel was surprised.

'Well, not on purpose!' exclaimed Rosemary impatiently, realising what she had said. 'It was yesterday, you see. Daddy suggested we should ride down to the village, and get some ice-cream.'

'When you were out riding?' Rachel probed, and the little girl expelled her breath in a noisy assent.

'How was I to know she would think he'd come to complain?' she asked frustratedly. 'I mean, Daddy never—ever—goes into the village stores. Mrs Moffat gets everything we want delivered.'

'I see.' Rachel was beginning to understand. 'And Mrs Reed spilled the beans, hmm?'

'Mmm.' Rosemary groaned. 'I s'pose it was me being with him, and Daddy asking her how Mr Reed was keeping. Mr Reed has bronc—broncy—a bad cough, and Daddy said he hoped he'd stopped smoking, because cigarettes make coughs worse.'

'And Mrs Reed thought he knew she had been supplying you with cigarettes.'

'I think so. Anyway, she got all flustered, and said she worried a lot about giving cigarettes to children, but that as he was such a good customer she didn't like to refuse.'

'The old——' Rachel had been about to say 'devil', but she managed to bite her tongue. 'So, what happened?'

Rosemary pulled a face. 'Well—Daddy was ever so polite. He didn't tell her he knew nothing about it, like I thought he would. He said he wouldn't send me to the shop for cigarettes ever again, and that he knew he could trust Mrs Reed not to say anything, because she might lose her licence if she did.'

'Neat.' Rachel couldn't prevent the wry smile that touched her lips at the little girl's words. So, Matthew had defended his daughter at last. And spiked Mrs Reed's guns into the bargain.

'That was then,' added Rosemary gloomily. 'But when we got home he was really angry. He said he had been having second thoughts about sending me to boarding-school—you know, like I told you before—but that if I was prepared to *steal* to defy him, perhaps he ought to think again.' She sniffed. 'I wasn't stealing really, was I? Mrs Reed knew what I was doing.'

Rachel hesitated. 'Yes. But you were asking her to put them on your father's account. He was paying for them, wasn't he? Not you.'

'Well, he buys me sweets and Colas all the time.'

'That's different, and you know it.'

Rosemary looked sulky. 'I thought you were my friend.'

'I am your friend. At least, I hope I am. But you have to admit, you were spending money that wasn't yours.'

Rosemary shrugged. 'Oh, well, it doesn't matter now,' she muttered moodily. 'He's hardly likely to give me a second chance.'

'I wouldn't say that.' Rachel regarded her gently. 'And don't say he, say Daddy. You're not going to get anywhere if you revert to being insolent.'

'What do you know about it?' Rosemary gave her a brooding look. 'You'll be leaving soon. Grandmama says so. She says that when you get back to London you'll soon forget all about me.'

'No, I won't.' Rachel knew a moment's irritation at the old lady who, deliberately or otherwise, was helping to give Rosemary such a complex. 'And don't expect the worst of everybody. Your father's had a difficult time, coping—coping with the funeral and everything. Maybe if you tried to understand his position, he'd find it easier to understand yours.'

'Do you think so?' Rosemary's face mirrored her uncertainty. 'He used to like me. At least, I thought he did. When I was little he used to play with me a lot. He even taught me to ride. But for ages now he's always been too busy when I've asked him to go riding with me, and he never takes me to see Auntie Helen and Uncle Gerry like he used to do before.'

'Helen and Gerald,' echoed Rachel softly, remembering Matthew's sister and her husband with some affection. They had not exactly been close friends when she was married to Matthew, but at least they hadn't turned against her when the marriage fell apart.

'Do you know them?' asked Rosemary at once, and Rachel instantly regretted her involuntary admission.

'I—used to,' she conceded, unwilling to explain exactly how she knew them. 'Um—you know, it's such a lovely morning, I think I might go for a walk. Do you want to come with me?'

Rosemary's small face brightened, and then grew doubtful again. 'Well—I'm supposed to stay indoors today,' she admitted slowly. 'Daddy said——'

'I would welcome your company,' put in Rachel temptingly, deciding that, no matter what Matthew thought, as long as she was here at Rothmere she would do what she could to make Rosemary's life a little more exciting. It didn't sound as if she had any fun in the normal course of events, and while Barbara's illness must have accounted for part of the problem it was by no means the whole solution. Something had gone wrong here, something more than the trauma created when one member of a family develops a terminal disease. Not that Rachel expected to find out exactly what that problem was, that wasn't her concern. But if by befriending the child she could help her and her father to understand one another better, then surely it was worth the effort?

'Well...' Rosemary was faltering. 'Perhaps if you *need* somebody to come with you...'

'Oh, I do.' Rachel smiled. 'How about if you show me your pony, hmm? The walk to and from the stables should be just about right.'

It was a good morning, and Rachel, just as much as Rosemary, enjoyed the outing. Meeting Jim Ryan again was quite an experience, and if the old Irishman thought it was odd that she and the child who had caused the break-up of her marriage should seem such good friends, he kept his opinion to himself. Instead, he expressed his pleasure at seeing her again, and asked how she was feeling after suffering such an accident.

'Sure, and you won't be wanting Jessica saddled this morning, will you?' he added ruefully. 'Not that she's used much these days anyway. But Mr Matt wouldn't have me get rid of her. You know, I think he's got some affection for the beast.'

Of course, Rosemary was curious to know when Rachel had ridden the old chestnut mare, but she managed to divert the girl by asking to see the other horses in the stables. Particularly the black stallion Matthew had been riding the afternoon they had met on Rothdale Pike. That proud animal, which Rosemary told her was named Saracen, snorted a little nervously when they approached his stall, and Jim Ryan was on hand to advise caution.

'Ah, but he's a fine creature, so he is,' Ryan nodded, dodging the stallion's nodding head. 'But I think he has an aversion to the ladies. Now, watch out, Rosie, his teeth are sharp.'

They walked back to the house in time for lunch, and to Rachel's relief—and Rosemary's too, no doubt—they didn't meet anyone on the way.

'We'll have to do this again,' Rachel said lightly, as they parted at the foot of the stairs, and the little girl nodded eagerly.

'Tomorrow?' she suggested, and Rachel made a gesture of assent.

'Why not?' she agreed, starting up the stairs towards her room. 'Come and see me after breakfast. That is, if your father has no objections.'

Rosemary's expression was eloquent of her feelings, and Rachel guessed they were both thinking the same thing. No one could be sure what Matthew's reaction might be, and if Lady Olivia found out Rachel had no doubt that she would object, very strongly.

The next morning, Dr Newman told her he was dismissing Nurse Douglas. 'Not that I want you to infer from this that I consider you completely recovered,' he added swiftly. 'But, in the circumstances, I don't believe her presence is warranted, particularly as Mr Conroy's staff are more than capable of providing the necessary care.'

'I see.' Rachel's tongue circled her upper lip. 'But— couldn't I return to the vicarage, then?'

'I wouldn't advise it.' The doctor was concerned. 'My
dear Mrs Conroy, my reasons for letting Nurse Douglas
go are as I have stated: because you are being adequately
cared for here. I can hardly endorse your returning to
your uncle's home, when by his own admission his wife
has more than enough to do already.'

Rachel hesitated, wondering who had told him that.
She could guess, but what she couldn't understand was
why Matthew seemed to be compelling her to stay. Even
so, she couldn't deny it was something of a relief not to
have to face the prospect of meeting Aunt Maggie's re-
criminations until she felt stronger.

Meanwhile, her friendship with Rosemary blossomed.
In spite of the fact that Matthew, and his mother, were
unaware of the relationship, Rachel couldn't find it in
her heart to send the little girl away. Besides, she consoled her conscience, they were doing no harm. And if
her company made this transitionary period easier for
the child, surely no one should complain?

In consequence, she became accustomed to
Rosemary's appearing in her room every morning, ready
and willing to escort her new-found friend on ex-
peditions about the estate. She didn't know what
Rosemary told Agnetha, or where the au pair thought
she was. But for Rachel herself they were voyages of
rediscovery, as she became reacquainted with the memories of her past.

Of course, there was a bittersweet quality to her memories, and it wasn't always easy to dissociate them from
the feelings she had shared with Matthew. But she knew
she might never have another chance to explore the
sometimes painfully familiar woods and gardens of
Rothmere, and she drank in the sights and sounds she
saw like a prisoner who was soon to be cut off from
them forever.

The weather had continued to be warm and dry, as if
making its own contribution to her recovery, and she
and Rosemary spent a lot of time down at the lake.
Rachel half wished they could take one of the small
dinghies they found in the boat-house out on to the water,

but it was years since she had sailed with Matthew, and she dared not take that responsibility.

However, it was appropriate that when Matthew found them it should be down at the jetty. They were sitting on the wooden boards, legs dangling over the water, trailing a line that Jim Ryan had given them in the hope that they might catch something. Not that it was likely, of course, and they had already agreed that if they did by some miracle catch a fish they would throw it back, but it was sufficiently absorbing an occupation for them not to be aware of anyone's approach until they felt the vibration of his footsteps on the planks.

'Um—Daddy!' exclaimed Rosemary in some alarm, scrambling to her feet with alacrity. 'What are you doing here? Grandmama said——'

She broke off at that point, belatedly realising how incriminating her words had been, and Rachel sighed. Until that moment she had remained where she was, refusing to allow Matthew's appearance to panic her into a display of the trepidation she was feeling, but now she felt obliged to get to her feet. It was her fault that Rosemary was here, and she was the one to be blamed.

'And what did Grandmama say?' Matthew was asking now, his lean frame propped against the wall of the boat-house, and Rachel's prepared response faltered in the face of the indulgence of his tone. He didn't look angry, she thought doubtfully, and he didn't sound angry. But could she trust his expression after the way he had behaved before?

'I—well—she said you had an—an appointment in—in town,' Rosemary stammered in reply. 'I—I have been doing some reading, honestly. Only—only Rachel needed some company, and—and I offered to show her around.'

'I see.'

Matthew's arms were folded, and he inclined his head, as if considering her explanation. He was dressed more formally today, Rachel noticed unwillingly. His dark blue suit of fine wool accentuated the width of his broad shoulders, and the narrow trousers enhanced his height and the muscled length of his legs. He looked as if he was indeed equipped for a business meeting in the city, and she wondered what had brought him here, so far off his usual route.

'I should say that what Rosemary says is true,' Rachel offered now, as the pregnant silence stretched. 'She—I—we have spent some time together. I'm sorry, if you don't approve, but I have been grateful for her company.'

'Did I say I didn't approve?' Matthew countered, lifting his head and looking at her with cool, appraising eyes.

'No, but...' Rachel thrust her hands into the back pockets of her jeans to hide their trembling uncertainty. 'I can't imagine any other reason why you might have come looking for us. Did—did Mr Ryan tell you where we were?'

Matthew regarded her steadily for a moment, and then he straightened and pushed his own hands into the pockets of his jacket. 'I didn't need anyone to tell me where you were,' he replied, turning his attention to the water. 'I've known what was going on for several days——'

'You have?' Rosemary interrupted them, her eyes wide. 'Did Grandmama——'

'As far as I know, your grandmother still thinks you spend every morning reading with Agnetha,' retorted Matthew flatly. 'But if you think *she* was prepared to take the responsibility for your absence, you're very much mistaken.'

Rosemary's jaw dropped. 'Agnetha told you?'

'Who else?'

'The mean thing——'

'It *is* her job,' replied Matthew reprovingly. 'Look, don't blame Agnetha. I didn't stop you, did I? You're still here.'

Rachel moistened her dry lips. 'Does that mean you have no objections to Rosemary and I spending time together, then?' she asked evenly. 'You must appreciate this is quite a surprise, after—after——'

'After the way I behaved before, I know.' Matthew's mouth thinned. 'But I had plenty of time to regret my actions, didn't I? And, contrary to popular belief, I don't get any pleasure out of hurting people.'

Their eyes met, and held, and this time it was Rachel who looked away. 'Well,' she said evenly, 'that's all right, then, isn't it?' She gave the little girl an encouraging look. 'Because we've become good friends, haven't we?'

Rosemary smiled. 'Yes. Yes, that's right, Daddy,' she agreed eagerly, obviously relieved at this unexpected turn of events. 'So you won't tell Grandmama, will you? I mean, she doesn't like Rachel, and she'd never understand.'

Matthew turned to his daughter. 'Did she say that? Grandmama, I mean. That she didn't like Rachel?' His eyes were intent.

'Well...' Rosemary looked a little uneasy now. 'Maybe not, exactly. But it's obvious, isn't it? You should hear the way she speaks to her!'

Rachel looked surprised now, and a frown drew Matthew's eyebrows together. 'What did you say?' he exclaimed. 'What have you heard your grandmother say that I haven't?'

Rosemary's face turned red. 'Not a lot,' she said, evidently regretting her impulsive outburst, but her father was not prepared to leave it there.

'Come on,' he invited, his tone hardening as he spoke. 'I'm waiting to hear how this revelation came about.'

'Oh, Daddy.' Rosemary looked utterly deflated now, and although Rachel felt sorry for her there was little she could do. 'It was just something I overheard Grandmama say when she went to visit Rachel when she was ill. You know how—how *cold* Grandmama can be.'

'I still don't understand how you heard what was said between Rachel and your grandmother,' replied Matthew tersely. 'Were you there?'

'No.' Rosemary hunched her shoulders. 'Not exactly.'

'What does that mean?'

'Oh, Daddy!'

'Rosemary.'

'Oh, all right.' She flung her hands out in front of her. 'I heard what she said as I was leaving.'

'You mean you eavesdropped outside the door,' amended her father shrewdly. 'Isn't that right? Isn't that what you did?'

'Lady Olivia was talking before Rosemary left the room,' Rachel put in quickly, trying to remember exactly what Matthew's mother had said. She had certainly brought up the subject of Rachel's not being prepared to have her son's baby, and she hoped Rosemary hadn't heard this, or, if she had, that she hadn't understood it.

Matthew's attention shifted. 'So,' he said, making an evident effort to control his impatience, 'you agree with Rosemary's assessment of my mother's attitude?'

'I didn't say that.' Rachel sighed. How quick he was to jump to conclusions. 'Matthew, you know as well as I do that your mother didn't want me here. If the child's picked that up, too, can you blame her?'

Matthew looked as if he was about to say something scathing, and then seemed to change his mind. With an obvious effort, he forced himself to relax, and both Rachel and Rosemary breathed a little more easily as he turned once more to rest his shoulder against the boat-house. 'OK,' he said, staring out across the water. 'I won't tell my mother what's been going on——'

'Oh, Daddy! *Thank you!*'

Without waiting for him to finish, Rosemary covered the space between them and wrapped her thin arms around his waist. And, looking at Matthew over his daughter's head, Rachel thought he was as surprised as she was at this unexpected display. Evidently embraces of this kind were not a common thing between them.

But Matthew's initial response was in the same spirit at least, even if the verbal response that followed was not what Rosemary had expected. His arms automatically closed about his daughter, hugging her to him warmly, and, watching them together, Rachel knew a treacherous feeling of envy. He should still have been her husband, and this should have been *their* daughter, she reflected bitterly, unable to tear her eyes away. Or their *son*, she amended, as remembrance knifed inside her.

'I want *you* to tell her.'

Matthew's words brought her abruptly back to the present, and she blinked a little confusedly herself as Rosemary uttered a disbelieving cry. 'You don't mean that!'

'I do.' Matthew held her, as she would have pulled away from him. 'I want you to tell Grandmama that you and Rachel are friends, and that I have no objections to your spending your free time with her.'

Rosemary's instinctive denial faltered. 'You mean you'll tell her you knew about what was going on?'

'I mean I won't tell her I didn't,' amended Matthew drily. 'But in future I want you to come to me if you have any—problem with Grandmama. I want us—you and me—to be like a family again.'

Rosemary's lips quivered. 'Do you mean that?'

'I've just said so, haven't I?'

'And—and what about——' she was obviously loath to say it, but she eventually got the words out '—going to boarding-school?'

Matthew looked across at Rachel, holding her eyes as he spoke. 'It's early days yet,' he said. 'We'll see how you behave over the next couple of months. I may revise my opinion and send you to a girl's day-school I know in Keswick. It's where your cousin Lucy goes, and she seems to like it.'

Rosemary gulped. 'And would I be a day girl, too?'

'If you behave yourself, I don't see why not,' replied her father, looking down at her now. 'But only if I hear no more reports of naughtiness from Agnetha. Or your grandmother either, if it comes to that.'

'You won't.' Rosemary was almost speechless. She caught back a sob. 'Can I go and tell Mrs Moffat?'

'Why not?'

Matthew smiled, and after another swift hug Rosemary released herself. 'Did you hear that?' she asked, turning to Rachel as she brushed an errant tear from her cheek. 'I'm going to go to Lucy's school. Daddy's not going to send me to boarding-school, after all.'

'That's wonderful news,' said Rachel warmly, despising herself for envying the child. If only her problems could be as easily solved as Rosemary's. Unfortunately, she didn't have anyone fighting on her side—least of all Matthew.

CHAPTER TWELVE

THERE was a distinct silence after Rosemary left them, and Rachel turned to watch the child's skipping departure to avoid Matthew's subjective gaze. She supposed she ought to have accompanied her, but Rosemary was obviously eager to get back to the house, and Rachel would have been an unnecessary encumbrance. All the same, it was difficult to know what to say now, and although she wanted to express her approbation at his decision she doubted he would be interested in hearing it.

'You approve, I take it,' he said at last, and now she was compelled to turn and face him.

'Of course,' she replied, lifting her shoulders in an expressive gesture. 'It's—it's what she needed; your—your belief in her.'

Matthew inclined his head. 'You think I didn't believe in her before, is that it?'

Rachel sighed. 'I don't know. I only know that—well, you didn't seem to have a lot of time for her be—before.'

'Before what?' Matthew moved nearer to her. 'Before Barbara died? Or before you came here?'

Rachel stood her ground. 'I don't flatter myself that my coming here had anything to do with it,' she declared, meeting his gaze with an effort. 'Maybe—maybe Barbara's illness obscured——'

'Barbara's illness didn't obscure anything,' retorted Matthew tautly. 'You could say it clarified a lot of things.' He didn't explain what he meant by this, but went on, 'My—relationship with Rosemary was in trouble long before Barbara was taken ill.' He shook his head. 'I'd almost forgotten what it was like to have a daughter.'

'You're very lucky to have her.' Rachel took a steadying breath. 'She's a very loyal little girl.'

'Do you think so?' Matthew seemed to be considering this. He took another step towards her. 'But you didn't like her much when you first met her, did you?'

Rachel sighed, and glanced behind her, grimacing at the dark expanse of water only a couple of feet away at the end of the jetty. Of all places to conduct a conversation, this must be the most unsuitable, she thought frustratedly. With Matthew between her and the shore, she was virtually his prisoner.

'Look, I've revised my opinion,' she said, edging alongside the boat-house. 'And I really am glad you've changed your mind about a boarding-school. I—I'm sure Barbara would have approved——'

'Barbara didn't give a damn what happened to Rosemary,' Matthew retorted harshly, putting out his arm and successfully blocking her exit. 'I thought you'd have realised that. Or did you think I was totally to blame for her irresponsibility?'

Rachel caught her breath. He was so close, and she wondered if he was aware of how much she was aware of him. He couldn't be, or he wouldn't be behaving like this, she thought unsteadily. Not after the way he had repelled any emotion between them the last time he had seen her. As she had wanted him to do, she reminded herself starkly. Dear God, just because the warmth and scent of his lean body was shudderingly familiar, there was no reason for her to lose sight of all reality...

'Will you let me pass?' she said now, forgetting for the moment that he had asked her a question, and he expelled a heavy breath.

'What's the matter?' he asked. 'Don't you want to believe that I'm not the unfeeling monster you've always painted me? Does it put a grain of doubt in your mind if I remind you that you were the one who used to tell me that Barbara could be both devious and self-motivating?'

'Stop it!' Rachel was forced to look up at him now, and she shivered at the look of weary resignation in his eyes. 'Barbara's been dead only three weeks! How can you talk about her like this?'

'Quite easily,' he said flatly, using his free hand to tuck a silken strand of honey-blonde hair behind her ear. His hand lingered against her flesh, and it was all she could do not to tilt her head against the hard brush of his fingers. 'You see, I never loved Barbara, and she certainly didn't love me. What I could give her, perhaps, but nothing else——'

'Don't!' Rachel pushed his hand away and tried to duck under his arm. But his arm dropped as she did, and instead of escaping him she was backed up against the warm wood of the boat-house wall. 'Matthew, you're going to regret this!'

'I regret it already,' he retorted, looking down at her with impassioned eyes. 'But I have to go to Geneva this afternoon, and I'm very much afraid you'll be gone by the time I get back.'

Rachel swallowed. 'You're going to be away for a few days?'

'Until next Tuesday or Wednesday, at the least,' he agreed, capturing her chin between his fingers. 'And while I was succeeding in convincing myself that I could let you leave here without making a fool of myself for a second time, I find that now there's an actual deadline to our separation I can't do it.'

'Matthew——'

'No, listen to me,' he muttered, bending his head and putting his mouth against the side of her neck. 'I want you to know I don't blame you for what happened——'

'Blame me?'

The terrible inertia that had been stealing over her at the touch of his lips was abruptly banished. That he should actually believe that she might welcome his advances was bad enough, but to suggest that she might blame herself for what had happened in the past was mortifying.

'Yes,' he was intoning now, his hand at her nape causing unwanted ripples of sensuality to invade her spine. 'For years I have blamed you. For years I swore that if I ever saw you again, I'd kill you! But although you might believe you can control your mind, you can never completely control your senses, and as soon as I saw you again I knew I'd been fooling myself all along——'

'Let go of me!' With a concerted effort, Rachel tore herself away from him, putting an arm's length between them, and staring at him with angry, disbelieving eyes. 'Don't touch me! Do you hear me? Don't you ever lay a hand on me again!' She caught back a sob. 'You say you don't blame me! My God, am I supposed to be grateful for that? What have you got to blame me for, that's what I'd like to know! I didn't do anything. *You did!* Do you need me to remind you what you did? Do you want me to tell you how I felt when I found you and Barbara—*my own cousin*!—together?'

Matthew's mouth was grim, but his emotions were still in command. Lunging forward, he grasped her wrist, and before she could formulate any resistance he had hauled her unceremoniously towards him. Her breasts, loose beneath the thin silk of her shirt, were crushed against his chest, and her legs bumped against his thighs. His breath was hot on her forehead as he wound the arm he had hold of behind her back, and, apparently uncaring that he might be hurting her, he trapped her effectively against him.

'You don't think before you speak, do you?' he snarled, glaring down at her. 'You never would listen to reason. You wouldn't even give me a hearing, before you ran away to London——'

'I didn't run away,' she got out painfully, but he obviously didn't believe her.

'I used to come and sit outside that apartment you took in Penrith, did you know that? Waiting for you to come out. But you never did, did you? At least, not while I was there. You were too scared to meet me face to face. Too scared to even pick up the telephone!'

'I wasn't scared,' she protested, wondering if he was aware that he was almost breaking her arm. Dear God, if he didn't let her go soon she was going to faint, and she had no wish to give him that satisfaction.

'What would you call it then?' he demanded now, and she took a gulping breath.

'How about—disgusted?' she choked, dredging up the last of her strength. 'Tell me, how long had it been going on before I found out? Barbara was already three months pregnant when I went away, which means that it has to have been——'

Her release was as sudden as her capture had been. One moment Matthew was holding her in a biting embrace, and the next he had uttered a savage interjection and let her go. So unexpectedly, indeed, that she was forced to clutch at him to save herself from falling off the jetty. Her fingers clawed desperately at his chest, tearing open the buttons of his shirt and finding purchase on the cloth. And, in so doing, the backs of her fingers came into contact with the warm skin of his midriff. But as soon as she felt his flesh against hers she dragged her hand away.

'What did you say?'

The violence of Matthew's tone was a welcome distraction to the wilful madness of her thoughts. Even though her shoulder was still stinging, as blood surged back into the tortured muscles, the sensuality of his warm body was a potent attraction. For a moment—for a heart-wrenching moment—she had known an almost uncontrollable impulse to go on touching him, and all the pain and anguish that lay between them had melted in the heat of that temptation. But it was only a physical aberration, she knew, born of her own frustrated emotions. And of her instinctive response to Matthew's sexuality...

'What did you say?'

She came to her senses a second time to find him staring at her with raw impatience. Evidently, he had repeated his question, and she had to blink away a certain incoherence as she struggled to remember what he meant.

'I—don't—know——'

'Barbara!' Matthew prompted grimly. 'You said Barbara was pregnant when you went away. Who told you that?'

Rachel blinked again. 'What do you mean? Who told me? It was a fact, wasn't it? What does it matter who——?'

'Because it wasn't true,' said Matthew savagely.

'Don't be stupid——'

'Don't you dare tell me not to be stupid!' he retorted angrily. 'For heaven's sake, Rachel, Barbara wasn't pregnant when you went away! Rosemary was born almost a year after the divorce! I want to know who told you Barbara was pregnant. Was it Barbara? God, I have to know the truth!'

Rachel backed away from him along the jetty, trying desperately to come to terms with what she had heard. 'But—Rosemary's ten years old,' she protested unsteadily, but Matthew shook his head.

'She's nine!' he told her flatly. 'Ask her how old she is, and she'll tell you.'

Rachel swallowed. 'Why should I believe you?'

'Don't be ridiculous! What would be the point of lying? You could easily find out when Rosemary was born. The records are there for everyone to see.'

Rachel put a trembling hand to her temple. 'But you did—you did—sleep with her, didn't you?' she got out unsteadily.

Matthew's nostrils flared. 'Yes.'

Rachel caught her breath. 'Oh, God!'

Matthew's mouth twisted. 'Don't you want to know *when*? Or *why*?'

Rachel shook her head. 'No——'

'Well, by God, you're going to,' declared Matthew harshly, going after her. 'And if you run away this time,

I'll go straight to your aunt and uncle and tell them how Barbara lied to get what she wanted.'

Rachel, who had reached the path that led up through a copse of trees, budding now with blossom, halted uncertainly. Then, even though all she really wanted to do was escape to the unguarded sanctuary of her room, she turned back.

'It—wasn't Barbara,' she admitted painfully. 'I—Aunt Maggie told me that Barbara was pregnant.'

'Good God!' Matthew made a sound that was a mixture of anger and anguish. 'And you believed her?'

'Why shouldn't I?' retorted Rachel swiftly. 'By your own admission, you and Barbara had been having an affair——'

'Not an *affair*!' Matthew shrugged off his jacket and thrust it roughly over his shoulder. 'Rachel, believe it or not, that night you—you found us, as you put it, was the first time we had ever—touched.'

'Oh, Matt, please——'

'Goddammit, it's the truth!' he swore angrily. 'And you had only yourself to blame! Or you would have, if you could see further than that selfish bloody nose of yours!'

'How dare you?'

'I dare, because it's the truth,' he stated. 'All right. You didn't want to have a baby. I was coming to terms with that——'

'Were you?'

'All right, I had my faults, too, but I was never deceitful——'

'Oh, Matt!'

'Never deceitful with you.'

Rachel shook her head. 'I don't know what you mean.'

'I think you do.'

'No, I don't.'

'All right,' he said again. 'When—when we had that first row, and I flushed the pills you were taking down the toilet, I thought you'd at least have *told* me if you'd started taking them again.'

Rachel stared at him uncomprehendingly. 'Yes. I would have.'

'But you didn't, did you?'

'Didn't what?'

'Tell me, dammit! You let me go on hoping that you might get pregnant, when all the time you were popping pills like there was no tomorrow!'

'That's not true!'

'It is true.'

Rachel caught her breath. 'It's not! I'm telling you now, I've never—I've never taken a contraceptive pill since—since you disposed of them.'

Matthew studied her grimly. 'Wait a minute. Let me backtrack a minute. Are you saying you've never knowingly tried to prevent a pregnancy since I destroyed your prescription?'

'That's right.' Rachel was trembling. *If he only knew,* she thought achingly, thinking of that still little body that had been taken from her...

'And—Maggie told you Barbara was pregnant?'

Rachel bent her head. 'Yes.'

'God!' Matthew rammed the heel of his hand hard against his forehead. 'So we both believed what we were told.'

Rachel licked her lips before looking up at him again. 'Not entirely,' she said unevenly. 'Don't forget, I had the evidence of my own eyes.'

'And so did I,' muttered Matthew savagely, scuffing his booted foot against the wooden piles of the jetty. 'That night you found us together, Barbara had shown me a half-used strip of contraceptive pills. She took them out of the drawer beside your bed.'

Rachel's lips parted. 'But—they weren't mine!'

'I didn't know that.'

Rachel stared at him in horror. 'But why didn't you ask me?'

'I was going to,' he declared bitterly. 'Only, if you remember, I never got the chance.'

Rachel tried to think. 'But when I found you——'

'I was stoned out of my mind!' exclaimed Matthew wearily. 'I don't know how much I drank that night. I don't remember too much of the night at all, after Barbara's revelation.' He expelled a heavy breath. 'I remember her saying what a pity it was that you seemed to care more about your career than me. I remember that. And I remember her mentioning that as long as you were taking the Pill you weren't likely to conceive, and I also remember arguing with her about it.'

'Oh, Matt.'

He frowned. 'Anyway, I know earlier in the evening we went upstairs to look in the drawer of the bedside cabinet, and the foil strip *was* there.'

'But she could have put it there at any time,' cried Rachel.

'I'm beginning to realise that now, but then——'

'You got drunk?'

'I suppose so. We went back to the library, and I remember my glass always seeming to be full, and Barbara sympathising with me, and smiling at me, and telling me how she would never do such a thing.'

Rachel felt sick. Even after all this time, his words still had the power to distress her.

'And when I came home?'

'I don't know.' He raked his hair back with a hand that was not quite steady. 'I suppose she must have suggested that I ought to be in bed and offered to help me undress.'

'Do you mean——?' Rachel could hardly say the words. 'Do you mean you hadn't slept together before I found you?'

'I don't think so.'

'You don't *think* so?'

'All right, then, *no*. We hadn't.' He shook his head. 'I doubt if I was capable of it.'

'That's some consolation, I suppose.' Rachel was bitter.

'Well, goddammit, if I had I'd have considered myself justified!' he replied unevenly. 'Rachel, I've never loved anyone as I loved you, and when I found out—*thought* I'd found out—that you'd been cheating on me——'

'You let Barbara offer you consolation!'

'Not until after you left,' Matthew countered harshly, and Rachel shivered.

'Left Rothmere?'

'Left *Penrith*,' corrected Matthew, with a scowl. 'That's how I know Barbara couldn't have been pregnant when you went away. But the night you went to London I decided I had nothing left to lose.'

'But why *Barbara*? Did you—did you *love* her?'

'Not love, no. I was grateful to her, I suppose, for exposing your duplicity, or what I thought was your duplicity, anyway. And she was there. And, dammit, I wanted to hurt you as you had hurt me!'

'Oh, Matt!'

'So now you know,' he muttered, coming closer to her. 'Does it make a difference?'

Rachel couldn't take it all in. She couldn't believe that everything that had happened could have pivoted on a lie—two lies, if she accepted that Barbara had tricked Matthew with what must have been her own contraceptive pills.

She looked up at Matthew, and her heart bled. Was it true? Had he really believed she had been lying to him? And why not, when she had been equally as eager to believe that he was having an affair with her cousin?

'Rachel . . .'

He put out his hand towards her, but she avoided his touch. However much she wanted to believe him, she had to have a little time to assimilate all she had learned, and what it might mean. And first of all she wanted to speak to Aunt Maggie. If what Matthew had said was true, then she had an awful lot to answer for.

'What's wrong?' he demanded now, his frustration plain, and her heart went out to him.

'Just—give me a little time to get used to the idea,' she begged, and, unable to resist the temptation, she put her hand on his sleeve. The flesh beneath the fine silk was taut and pulsing with life, and she knew an urge to bend her head and brush her lips against his warm skin.

'God—Rachel!' he groaned, as aware as she was of the chemistry between them, but the remembrance of Barbara, and what she had done to both of them, was a compelling deterrent. 'Look,' he added harshly, 'you know I don't have a lot of time. I'm leaving in——' he cast a swift look at his watch '—about half an hour. I wish I could postpone the trip now, but perhaps it's a blessing in disguise. By the time I get back, you'll have had time to decide what you want to do. At least promise me you'll stay until I get back. I need your assurance that you won't run out on me again.'

Rachel moistened her lips. 'All right.'

Matthew expelled a heavy sigh. 'You mean that?'

'Yes.' Rachel looked down at her hand on his sleeve, and then, throwing caution to the wind, she leant forward and kissed his cheek. 'Have a good journey,' she whispered. 'Take care.'

It was late in the afternoon when Rachel arrived at the vicarage. It had been difficult to get away from Rothmere without attracting undue attention, and she would have preferred no one to know where she was going. As it was, she had had to prevail on the old butler's kindness to enable her to borrow one of the estate's vehicles, but at least the mud-spattered Land Rover he had provided had not aroused the curiosity Matthew's Range Rover might have done.

In spite of the extreme tension she was feeling, driving again had not been a hazard. Indeed, she was amazed at her own resilience, after the body-blow of Matthew's revelations. She suspected the shock of what she had learned hadn't really hit her yet, and that the courage it was taking to come and confront her aunt was being sustained by the artificial amount of adrenalin in her system; but it had to be done. There was no way she could dismiss what Matthew had told her and look only to the future. If they were to have any future at all, she had to dispose of the skeletons of the past, and unless she saw Aunt Maggie face to face she would never know the truth.

Her aunt was in the sitting-room. Too late, Rachel remembered that the Young Wives had their regular weekly meeting at the vicarage on Friday afternoons, and the sound of perhaps a dozen female voices jarred her determination. But, after making no attempt to disguise her entry into the house, she was obliged to show her face, and she steeled herself against the stares that accompanied her appearance.

'Why—Rachel!' Her aunt's tone was at once surprised and wary. 'You should have let us know you were coming.'

'Yes.' But Rachel knew that was the last thing she would have done. She had wanted to catch her aunt unawares, and unprepared, but now the older woman was having plenty of time to consider why her niece had appeared.

'Why don't you sit down and join us?' Aunt Maggie invited, struggling to behave as the vicar's wife should. 'Girls, you all know my niece, Rachel Barnes, don't you? She came for dear Barbara's funeral, and, unfortunately, she had an accident while she was playing with Rosemary.'

That was hardly accurate, but Rachel was relieved not to have to go into further details. She acknowledged the ripple of restrained sympathy—some of it from girls she and Barbara used to go to school with—with polite gratitude, and then, excusing herself from the gathering, she offered to make some tea.

'That won't be necessary,' said her aunt swiftly, nodding at the cups on the table in front of them. 'We've had tea, haven't we, girls? I'm sure we'd all prefer to hear about the exciting job you have in London, instead. Rachel's an assistant producer, aren't you, dear? Very career-minded, our Rachel. Always was.' She met her niece's eyes. 'Always will be.'

'I wouldn't bank on that, if I were you,' said Rachel, equally as smoothly, and she saw her aunt's jaw sag for a moment.

But the aberration was brief, and Maggie quickly recovered. 'Well, I'm sure you know your own business best,' she remarked evenly. 'But it's a pity we can't all be as happy as Barbara and Matthew used to be. Poor Barbara! I don't know how Matt's going to manage without her. He's been totally devastated since she died.'

There was another murmur of sympathy from the women gathered in the room, and Rachel felt her nails digging painfully into her palms. With a few words, her aunt had altered the whole atmosphere of the meeting, and there was no doubt at all that the change had been deliberate.

However, not all the women present had regarded Barbara as the saint her mother was implying she had been, and one of them, Gillian Wyatt, got abruptly to her feet.

'I think it's time we were leaving,' she said, breaking up the meeting. 'It's obvious that Rachel would like to speak to her aunt alone, and it is nearly four o'clock. Time we were getting home and making ourselves useful to our husbands.'

'Oh, but I'm sure Rachel——' began Maggie urgently, but already two or three of the others were on their feet.

'Gill's right,' said Nancy Cullen, buttoning her cardigan. 'I know you're too polite to ask us to leave, but I'm sure you'd like to have a quiet word with your visitor. After all, it's been too long since Rachel visited the valley. We should see you more often, Rachel. It's not that far from London to Rothside.'

Rachel was quite touched by the way so many of the women took it upon themselves to wish her well as they were leaving. She had thought she would be regarded as the pariah in their midst, but it seemed that in this respect also she had been wrong. No one appeared to blame her for what had happened, or, if they did, they were prepared to keep their thoughts to themselves.

But when she and her aunt were alone she met an entirely different reaction. Maggie was grim and aggressive, and obviously of the opinion that the best method of defence was attack.

'Well?' she said, coming back into the sitting-room, where Rachel had been waiting while she said goodbye to her guests. 'What do you want? I hope you're not going to ask me if you can stay.'

'I'm not.' Rachel pushed her hands into the pockets of her jeans, and endeavoured to take control of the conversation. 'As a matter of fact, I don't want anything from you but some answers. Like, for instance, why you told me Barbara was pregnant when she wasn't.'

Maggie's thin face blanched. 'I beg your pardon?'

'You heard what I said, Aunt Maggie. Why did you tell me Barbara was pregnant——?'

'What are you talking about?' The older woman was blustering now. 'Why did I tell you Barbara was pregnant? I told you because she *was* pregnant, that's why. She and Matt—well, you know as well as I do what happened——'

'I know what *you* told me happened,' retorted Rachel harshly, and Maggie took a step back.

'What do you mean?'

'Oh, don't pretend you don't understand, Aunt Maggie. You understand very well. Only you never expected I would hear the truth, did you? You knew I was so upset over what I'd seen—what I *thought* I'd seen—that I'd believe anything. *Anything!*'

Her aunt swallowed. 'I don't know what this is all about, I really don't. Coming here, shouting about me lying to you. I haven't lied to you. Why should I?'

'Because you gambled that I'd believe you,' said Rachel tremulously. 'You guessed that if Barbara came to me with that story, I'd have been suspicious. That I might have asked Matt about it. But you—you knew I'd never expect you to *lie!*'

'And I didn't.' Her aunt stared at her with resentful eyes. 'How dare you even suggest such a thing? Just because Matt's a widower now, and you think you might have some chance of rekindling the past. You're getting older. You're beginning to regret what you lost——'

'Oh, I regret it, all right,' choked Rachel bitterly. 'And Matt does, too. He told me.'

'Matt told you——?' For a moment, Maggie was nonplussed. However she had thought Rachel might have learned of the deception, she had evidently not expected it to have been from him.

'Yes, Matt,' said Rachel contemptuously, pursuing her objective. 'He told me the truth. The whole truth. How he had nothing to do with Barbara in a sexual way until I left the district. That Barbara couldn't possibly have been pregnant, and that Rosemary isn't *ten* years old, she's *nine*!'

Maggie blinked, and Rachel could almost find it in her heart to feel sorry for her. It must have been hard to justify the lies she had told to herself, even if they had been to help Barbara. And, although she had never liked Rachel, surely she had not hated her enough to do what she had done without coercion?

But even as these thoughts superimposed themselves upon her consciousness, her aunt spoke again. 'You're a fool, Rachel,' she said scornfully, and Rachel could sense the returning confidence in her voice. 'Matt's told you the truth, has he? He's told you that Barbara wasn't expecting his child when you went away, and you believed him because Rosie is only nine years old!' She gave a harsh laugh. 'He didn't tell you about the miscarriage she had, I suppose? He didn't tell you that Barbara lost their first baby only weeks before it was due!'

'That's not true!'

Rachel's response was instinctive, born of the desire to silence her aunt's accusing voice, but Maggie was not finished.

'It is true,' she retorted. 'And if you don't believe me, ask your uncle. He wouldn't lie to you, would he? Not Uncle Geoff! Not the man who gave you a home at the expense of his own family!'

CHAPTER THIRTEEN

'You've got a visitor, Rachel.' Alan Maxwell stopped beside her desk and quirked a mocking eyebrow in her direction. 'Does Justin know you've been investigating the aristocracy for this new lifestyles format he's creating?'

'What?' Rachel lifted her head wearily, not really in the mood for her young colleague's provocation. She had a mountain of work to get through before the airing of that evening's programme, and with Justin breathing down her neck every five minutes she was in no state to indulge in verbal sparring with the man who wanted her job.

'I said—does Justin know——?'

'Yes, I heard that.' Rachel endeavoured not to let her tension show. It wouldn't do to give Alan another reason to complain to Justin that she simply wasn't doing her job. 'You mentioned something about the—aristocracy?'

'That's right.' Alan jerked his head towards one of the empty studios. 'I've put her in there. You'd better go and sort it out before she really sets the station by its ears.'

Rachel put down her pen. 'Sort who out?' she asked evenly.

'She calls herself Lady Olivia—Conroy. Funny that. I never realised before. It's the same name as yours.'

Rachel felt as if all the blood were draining out of her body. Lady Olivia? Here? Her hands curled convulsively on the desk in front of her. What was Lady Olivia Conroy doing in London? And why had she come to see her? What possible reason could have brought her here?

'Are you all right?'

Even Alan, uncaring of her feelings as he usually was, had noticed her pallor, and Rachel made a determined effort to allay his curiosity. If he went to Justin now and told him that Matthew's mother had come here to see her, who knew what further catastrophe that might precipitate?

As it was, she and Justin were barely on speaking terms, his reaction to her return to work four months ago very much tempered by her present lack of any enthusiasm. He had no sympathy with her, she knew, and she had never attempted to explain what had happened at Rothside to him. But she had no doubt that he had guessed that Matt was at least in part to blame for her loss of co-ordination, and it was only their long association that was preventing him from replacing her.

But it was incredibly difficult to apply herself to anything at the moment, and she was seriously thinking of giving up her job at the television station and finding something less demanding to employ her time. Where once she had looked forward to coming to work, now she loathed even getting out of bed in the mornings, and her whole life seemed empty and without any point.

She had believed that she couldn't feel any worse than she had when she'd first come to London ten years ago, but that had been proved to be as untrue as everything else. Wounds that had at least partially healed did not take kindly to being opened again, and, although once she would have said that Matthew couldn't hurt her any more, now she recognised this for the fiction it was.

She should have left well alone, she thought bitterly. No matter how convincing Matthew's words had sounded, she should never have attempted to verify the past. It should have been enough that he had *told* her his side of the story. Without her aunt's involvement, they could have been happy.

Or could they? For weeks after her return to London Rachel had asked herself that question without coming up with any satisfactory answer. If she had not approached Aunt Maggie, would the woman have let them be happy? Or would she have chosen to wait until they had a child of their own before exposing Matthew for the liar he was?

In any event, she had not waited to find out. Once Uncle Geoff had conceded, albeit a little bemusedly, that Barbara had indeed lost a baby before Rosemary was born, Rachel had only wanted to escape. She had been sorry to leave Rosemary, particularly as she had been unable to tell the little girl when, or even *if*, they would ever see one another again. But it was imperative that she get away before Matthew returned from Geneva, and although she had wondered if he might come after her, as he had done before, she had heard nothing more from him.

And now this. Her stomach quivered at the thought of Matthew's mother sitting in the empty studio, waiting to speak to her. And for what purpose? What earthly reason could have brought Lady Olivia to London? Rachel knew the old lady had friends in town, but she couldn't believe that this was just another social call. She and Lady Olivia didn't have—had never had—that kind of an association.

'Do you want me to get rid of her?' Belatedly, Alan showed an unexpected compassion. Perhaps even he could see how unnerved his news had made her, and the stark pain in the eyes she raised to his face made him shift a little uncomfortably. 'I can tell her you're too busy,' he offered. 'I could even tell her you're not here. Why don't you take an early lunch? It's cold outside, but the sun is warm.'

'No.' Rachel looked down at the papers on her desk again and shook her head. 'No, it's all right. I'll see her,' she said, sliding back her chair and getting to her feet on legs that were distinctly shaky. 'But—thanks for the offer. I'll do the same for you some time.'

Alan looked as if he half regretted his leniency, but he said no more as she ran a nervous hand over her hair and checked that there were no specks of lint on her skirt. The dark green velvet suit she was wearing unfortunately enhanced her pallor, and she thought how haggard she looked when she caught a glimpse of her reflection in the swing glass doors.

Lady Olivia was not *sitting* waiting for her. When Rachel entered the small studio, which was used for recording interviews for their radio channel, she found the old lady standing stiffly by the windows, staring out on to the roofs below with a definite air of tension. But she turned when she heard the door open, and her knuckles tightened perceptibly on the bag she held in her hands.

Rachel squared her shoulders, unconsciously adopting a defensive stance. But she could still think of no good reason why Lady Olivia should be here, and she automatically anticipated the worst.

'Good morning,' she said, her words tight, her features schooled and impassive. 'I understand you wish to see me.'

Lady Olivia regarded her silently for several seconds, and then, as if no longer capable of maintaining her indifference, her shoulders sagged. 'May I sit down?'

'Of course.' Rachel shook off a sense of unreality, and nodded towards a chair. 'Please.' She paused as the old lady took the seat. 'Can I get you some coffee?'

'Perhaps. Later,' said Matthew's mother, fingers that were not quite steady loosening the buttons of her tweed jacket. 'There.' She sighed. 'That's better. I was beginning to think you had refused to see me.'

Rachel could feel the sense of unreality returning, and frowned. 'I beg your pardon?'

'I said, I was beginning to think you had refused to see me.' Lady Olivia's thin lips parted in a faint smile. 'But you always were a polite child, weren't you, Rachel? Even if people were not always polite to you.'

Rachel wondered if she had been working too hard, and that this little scene was simply a figment of her imagination. Perhaps she was dreaming, she thought. Perhaps she would wake up soon and discover she was late for work again. Justin had already complained about her tardy timekeeping. He had even asked her if she was trying to get him to sack her...

'I know I must be the last person you expected to see.' Lady Olivia's voice came again, as if from a distance, and Rachel struggled to concentrate on what she was saying. 'I must admit, six months ago, I would have agreed with you. But circumstances alter cases, as they say, and I find my son's happiness is more important than my pride.'

Rachel stared at her. 'I'm afraid I——'

'You don't know what I'm talking about, do you?' Lady Olivia didn't wait for her to shake her head before continuing, 'No, well, I dare say that's not so surprising. I haven't exactly welcomed you to Rothmere in the past.'

'Lady Olivia——'

'Please, won't you sit down, too? What I have to say will not take long, but I find myself faltering these days, and with you standing over me like this——'

Rachel expelled a breath. 'Did Matthew send you here?' she asked abruptly, without any emotion, a possible excuse for the old lady's being here suddenly occurring to her. 'Because if he did——'

'Matt doesn't know I'm here,' the old lady replied wearily. 'You have my word on that. Indeed, I would go so far as to say that he would be furious if he knew. But, unhappily, that is not likely, and——'

'*Unhappily?*'

'Yes. Oh——' Lady Olivia spread her hands '—won't you sit down, Rachel? I can't go on looking up at you like this. It makes my head swim, and I have to keep my senses.'

Rachel hesitated a moment, and then, reluctantly, drew forward another of the leather-based chairs and subsided into it. 'All right,' she said. 'I'm sitting. What is it you want to tell me?'

Lady Olivia's fingers smoothed the fabric of her skirt, pleated the wool repeatedly, and then, just as Rachel was on the verge of springing frustratedly to her feet again, she said, 'I want you to come back to Rothmere.'

'*What?*' Rachel felt a surge of adrenalin coursing through her veins, and how she prevented herself from thrusting back the chair and walking out of the studio, she never knew. 'You're not serious?'

'I am serious.' Lady Olivia lifted her head and looked at her now. 'Matt needs you, Rachel. Rosemary needs you, too, I think. And *I* need you.' Her lips twisted. 'Oh, don't look like that, I've not entirely lost my reason. What I'm saying is, I need you because Matt needs you. If you don't come back, I'm very much afraid I'll lose him.'

Rachel blinked. 'Lose him?' she echoed. 'What do you mean, lose him?'

Lady Olivia heaved a sigh. 'Well—ever since the accident, he's been drinking——'

'Accident?' Rachel's mouth dried. 'What accident?'

'Rosemary's accident. But you know about that.'

'No, I don't.'

'You don't know she had a fall from Saracen?'

'No!' Rachel was horrified. 'How could I?'

'But—well, didn't your uncle write and tell you——?'

'No one wrote to me,' Rachel cut in swiftly. 'What happened? Is she all right? Good lord, *Saracen*! That's her father's horse, isn't it?' She remembered the huge black stallion with awful apprehension.

'Yes, that's right.' Lady Olivia shook her head. 'The little idiot should never have got on its back. But when Matthew came home and found you'd gone back to London, he became totally unapproachable, and I suppose Rosemary was trying to attract his attention.'

'Oh, God!' Rachel felt sick. 'Was she—was she badly hurt?'

'Fortunately not badly.' Lady Olivia grimaced. 'She had cuts and bruises, of course, and like you she had some concussion. But I'm afraid her ruse—if that's what it was—to get Matt's attention backfired. If anything, since the accident he's been even more withdrawn, and when Malloy told me how much he was drinking——'

Rachel's hands clenched. 'What makes you think I can do anything to help him?' she asked, fighting the instinctive urge to throw common sense aside and go and see Matthew for herself.

'Who else is there?' replied Lady Olivia bitterly. 'It was you he always wanted. He would never listen to anyone else.'

'How can you say that?' Rachel couldn't prevent the uncontrollable retort. 'He lied to me——'

'When? When did he lie to you?' Lady Olivia stared at her fiercely. 'If he told you he never loved Barbara, then it's the truth. He's not lying. After the first few months, their marriage was just a sham. If it hadn't been for Rosemary...' Her voice trailed away, and she fumbled in her handbag for a tissue as Rachel took several steadying breaths.

'It wasn't that,' she said at last, realising she at least owed it to this woman to be honest. 'I don't know if Matt ever loved Barbara. He was certainly attracted to her——'

'Not until you went away,' the old lady asserted swiftly. 'You didn't really believe he had been unfaithful to you, did you? My God, that night he found out you had been cheating him, he was too drunk to—well, you know what I mean.'

Rachel's features felt frozen. 'Is that what he told you?'

'Eventually,' agreed Lady Olivia. 'After I confronted him with it. Mrs Moffat found the bottles the following morning. It wasn't until later that I found out Barbara had been involved.'

Rachel got up now, unable to sit still any longer. 'I—wasn't cheating on him,' she said at last, walking to the windows and rubbing her elbows with nervous hands. 'Barbara—I think Barbara made that up to cause trouble between us. In any event, she achieved her objective, didn't she? And picked up the pieces into the bargain.'

Lady Olivia caught her breath. 'Are you saying you were not opposed to having a baby?'

'No. Yes. Oh, in the beginning I was, but after-wards...' Rachel shook her head. 'All I'm saying is, they weren't my pills that Barbara showed Matt. They must have been hers.'

'And when did you learn all this?'

'Matt told me,' said Rachel dully. 'The day before I left Rothmere.'

'And it didn't mean anything to you?'

Rachel swung round. 'Of course it meant something to me. But it wasn't enough.'

Lady Olivia lifted her thin shoulders. 'I hoped—I had hoped—that you still cared for my son.'

'It's a little late for that, isn't it?'

'I'm beginning to think it is.' The old lady looked drained.

'In any case,' Rachel couldn't let it alone, 'even if I did still care about Matt, I couldn't live with a liar.'

'You said that before.' Lady Olivia blinked. 'In what way did Matt lie to you? I've told you he didn't love Barbara——'

'And I've said it wasn't that.'

'Then what was it?'

Rachel was trembling now, but she couldn't help it. 'He—he told me Barbara wasn't pregnant when I left Penrith.'

'She wasn't.' Lady Olivia frowned.

'She was.'

'No.' Lady Olivia shook her head. 'I can assure you——'

'If you're going to say that Rosemary is only nine years old, I already know that. But Barbara had a miscarriage, didn't she?'

'Well—yes——'

'There you are, then.' Even now, the confirmation made her feel sick.

'But it was after they were married, my dear. And the foetus was barely two months old.'

'No!' Rachel couldn't believe it. She *wouldn't* believe it. Her uncle had endorsed everything Aunt Maggie had said, and he wouldn't have lied to her.

'I'm afraid it's yes.'

'It can't be.' Rachel shook her head.

But what had Aunt Maggie said exactly? she asked herself desperately. How had she phrased the question? She had asked Uncle Geoff, on Rachel's behalf, whether it was true that Barbara had been pregnant before her marriage, and Uncle Geoff had said yes. And then she had gone on to ask whether Barbara had had a miscarriage, and—and—— Rachel put an unsteady hand to her head. And—she had jumped to the obvious conclusion, just as Aunt Maggie had known she would.

She must have groaned, because Lady Olivia got up then, and came to put an anxious hand on her arm. 'Are you all right, Rachel?' she asked, her tone concerned, and Rachel knew an overwhelming urge to confide in the old lady.

'I—I—when Aunt Maggie told me Barbara had had a miscarriage, she said it had happened just—weeks before the baby was due.'

'Good lord!' Lady Olivia was astounded. 'But—why did you believe her? Did she offer you any proof?'

Rachel shook her head. 'No. No, she didn't. But she did ask Uncle Geoff to confirm it, and—and he did.'

'That the baby was only weeks from being due?' Lady Olivia looked aghast. 'I always thought Geoffrey Barnes was a foolish man, but I never thought he would betray his calling.'

'No. No, he didn't.' Rachel struggled to get some order into her words. 'But, you see, Matt hadn't told me about the miscarriage——'

'Because it wasn't important.'

'It was to me.' Rachel bent her head. 'Anyway, when—when Uncle Geoff agreed that Barbara had lost a baby, I didn't pursue it. It—it was enough, don't you see? As—as Aunt Maggie knew it would be.'

'That woman!' There was a wealth of dislike in Lady Olivia's voice. 'How your uncle has lived with her all these years, I'll never know.'

Rachel shook her head. 'I have to think——'

'Yes. Yes, I understand that.' Lady Olivia nodded now, and then, as another thought struck her, she added, 'There is one other point I think you should consider.'

'Yes?' Rachel was wary.

'Well,' said Lady Olivia, with the air of one who has just discovered something everyone else has overlooked, 'you might ask yourself how Barbara could have got pregnant at that point if she herself was using those pills you spoke about.'

CHAPTER FOURTEEN

IT WAS dark by the time she reached Rothmere, and the doubts Rachel had been nurturing during the latter part of the journey flourished anew as she turned between the familiar stone gateposts.

Although the roads had not been particularly busy once she had passed the Birmingham interchange, it had been after four o'clock before she could get away, and even then she had had to leave her apartment in some disorder. She had packed one suitcase, only to discover it was filled with shoes and underwear, so that she was obliged to tip everything out on to her bed and start again. But at that time her brain had simply not been functioning on any level beyond the basic one of getting to Matthew, and she guessed that if Lady Olivia had had any idea of the state she was in she would not have agreed to spend the night in London.

Justin had recognised defeat when he saw it, although he had, characteristically, been the one to kindle her misgivings. 'What makes you think Conroy will want you back, after you were so obviously willing to believe the worst of him?' he enquired, voicing thoughts Rachel would have preferred to leave unquestioned. 'After all, it isn't the first time you've walked out on him, is it? You might just find he's not prepared to take you back.'

Of course, he had been right, but at that time she had still been convinced that what she was doing was right. Now she was not so sure, and her hands clenched convulsively around the wheel of her car as she drove rather erratically towards the house.

It was a chilly September evening, and when she stepped out of the car the wind off the lake penetrated the folds of the cape she had wrapped around her. She had not stopped to change, and she was still wearing the dark green velvet suit she had worn to the studios, although now she felt dishevelled, and tired from the journey.

There were few lights visible in the house, and she wondered what she would do if Matthew was not at home. Lady Olivia had assured her that he seldom went out these days, but that was not to say he was a hermit. He could easily have decided to spend the night with some friends after his mother had left for London. Particularly as Lady Olivia had dropped Rosemary off at her daughter's on her way to see Rachel, and had explained that Agnetha had long since returned to Sweden.

Watkins answered her tentative ring, his old eyes widening at the sight of her. 'Why—Mrs Conroy!' he exclaimed, and Rachel managed a warm smile for his uncomplicated welcome. 'This is a pleasant surprise. Does Mr Matthew know you're coming?'

Rachel's smile faltered. 'No. No, he doesn't,' she admitted, glancing anxiously beyond him. 'Um—he is in, isn't he? I—I haven't made a wasted journey?'

'No. No, of course not.' But as Watkins stepped back to let her into the hall, his face mirrored his uncertainty. 'It's just that—well, Mrs Conroy, if he's not expecting you . . .'

Rachel could guess what he was thinking. If what Lady Olivia had confided was true, Matthew was seldom sober after six o'clock, and poor Watkins would be dreading the prospect of approaching him.

'It's all right,' she said now, patting the old man on the arm. 'You don't have to announce me. Is he in the library?' And at Watkins' nod, 'OK. Just leave it to me. I'll take the responsibility.'

'But Miss Rachel——'

Watkins evidently felt it was his duty to warn her what she might find, but Rachel shook her head. 'Don't worry,' she said firmly. 'If he throws me out, you can come and pick up the pieces.' She forced a light laugh. 'Honestly, it'll be all right. Lady Olivia knows I'm here.'

'Does she?'

The voice was harsh, but painfully familiar, and Rachel's brief spurt of humour expired. Although she had not thought she and Watkins were speaking loud enough to be overheard by anyone, Matthew's hearing was apparently sharper than she had thought. While she had been struggling to reassure the butler, he had wrenched open the library door, and now he stood regarding them with wary speculation.

Rachel had thought she was prepared for anything. Ever since her doubts about coming here had begun to plague her, she had played every possible scenario she could think of in her mind. Anger, resentment, bitterness, remorse. Anxious as she was, she had nevertheless believed that she could cope with any situation. She had even steeled herself to face his possible rejection. But what she had not anticipated was the shock that his appearance would generate. Even four months ago she had not been faced with anything like this.

For Matthew looked *ill*. There was no other word to describe him, and for the first time she realised why Lady Olivia had been desperate enough to come to London. The old lady had not been exaggerating when she had expressed her fears of losing her son. Looking at him now, Rachel could hardly believe that she had contributed to this change.

He was so thin, she thought worriedly, noticing how his clothes hung on him. There didn't appear to be any flesh on him anywhere, and his face was gaunt and shadowed with beard, his eyes red-rimmed and hollow.

'I said—does she?' he repeated now, supporting himself with one hand against the frame of the library door. 'I wondered where the old girl had gone.' His lips twisted. 'Where is she? I want to tell her exactly what I think of her!'

'Matt...'

Rachel glanced awkwardly at Watkins, but evidently Matthew had no qualms about involving the old butler in the proceedings. 'You can show—Miss Barnes out again, Watkins,' he stated, ignoring Rachel's tentative greeting. 'And, in future, you'd better ask me before inviting—*undesirables* into the house.'

'Oh, Mr Matt——'

'It's all right, Watkins.' Rachel realised she had to take charge of the situation before it got completely out of hand. 'I can show myself out, if necessary. You go and get on with your supper——'

'Don't you tell my staff what to do!' snarled Matthew, swaying a little as he pushed himself away from the door, and Rachel could smell the alcohol on his breath. 'You— get out of here right now. *Right now!*'

It took some doing, but Rachel turned her back on him and spoke once again to the butler. 'Go on, Watkins,' she directed, giving him an encouraging look. 'And tell Mrs Moffat we'd like some coffee, please. Black coffee. For two.'

'You've got a bloody nerve!' roared Matthew, as Watkins took one look at his employer and then hurried off to do Rachel's bidding. 'Coming here uninvited, giving your orders. Who the hell do you think you are?'

'I'm the woman who loves you,' said Rachel steadily, nodding towards the lamplit room behind him. 'Now, do we go into the library and talk about it? Or would you rather we conducted our conversation out here, with an uninvited audience?'

Matthew's mouth went slack. 'What did you say?' he muttered. And then, as if convinced he had misunder-stood what she had said, he shook his head a little blankly. 'No,' he added. 'Don't tell me. I don't want to know. I just want you to get out of here. I don't need anybody's pity, least of all yours.'

'It's not pity,' said Rachel quietly. 'Look, can't we just talk about this in private? I have come quite a long way.'

Matthew's mouth hardened. 'No one asked you to.' He scowled. 'I didn't ask you to, anyway.'

'I know that.' Rachel took a steadying breath. 'Please.'

'Please what?'

'Please can we go into the library and talk about this?'

'There's nothing to talk about.' Matthew's hand came up to support himself again as he almost lost his balance, and he rested his forehead on the muscled length of his forearm. 'God, Rachel, haven't you done enough? Did you have to do what the old lady asked you? God knows, you've never done it before.'

Rachel sighed. 'If I'd known you were in this state——'

'Yes? Yes?' He lifted his head sardonically. 'What would you have done? Come rushing back here to console me?' He grimaced. 'Like you did when Rosemary almost broke her neck?'

Rachel shook her head. 'I didn't know about Rosemary's accident——'

'And you professed to care about her,' he muttered, not listening to what she had to say. 'You know, you had her fooled, just like you fooled me. I really thought we were beginning to get somewhere before I went away. And then what happened? I come back, and find you've gone—just as you did before.' He groaned. 'God, I wanted to kill you!'

'Matt, I didn't know,' she insisted fiercely, and now he did hear her.

'Didn't know? Didn't know what? That I was crazy about you? That I'd always been crazy about you? Of course you did——'

He was talking in the past tense, and Rachel felt helpless. 'Rosemary's accident,' she cut in desperately. 'Matt, I didn't know she had had an accident. No one— no one told me.'

Matthew frowned, obviously trying to concentrate on what she was saying. 'You mean—Barnes never wrote and told you?'

'No.'

Matthew looked savage for a moment, but then he lifted his shoulders in an indifferent gesture. 'Oh, well,' he said carelessly, 'it's par for the course, isn't it? It's probably just as well. If you'd come back just then, I probably would have strangled you.'

'Oh, Matt!' Rachel heaved a deep breath. 'I know I've been stupid. I know you have every reason to be angry with me. But I did have my reasons, and if you'd only listen to me I could explain. After all, you didn't try to get in touch with me again, did you? How do you know I didn't think it was because you regretted what you had said?'

Matthew stared at her for a long moment, and then he licked his dry lips. 'I need a drink,' he said, lurching back into the library, and Rachel took the opportunity to follow him. Closing the door behind her, she moved quickly to put herself between him and the tray of bottles on the bureau.

'You don't need a drink,' she declared, resisting the angry aggression in his eyes. 'Don't you see? We have to talk to one another.'

'What about?'

'Us.'

'There is no "us",' he said flatly. 'Not any more.'

'Yes, there is.' Rachel refused to be daunted. 'Unless you're telling me you don't want me any more. Is that what you're saying?' She held her breath. 'Well? Is it?'

He turned away from her then, running unsteady hands through the tangled darkness of his hair, and her heart went out to him. He looked so lost and troubled, and she badly wanted to put her arms around him. But her courage was not that strong, no matter what Lady Olivia had said.

'You wouldn't be here if it weren't for my mother,' he muttered, after a long pause. 'You walked out of here of your own free will. Nothing's changed.'

'Yes, it has.' Rachel caught her lower lip between her teeth. 'Didn't you ever ask yourself why I might have gone away?'

Matthew's lips twisted. 'Oh, yes,' he said harshly. 'Yes, I asked myself that. But there was no answer, was there?

I'd told you my side of the story, but evidently it wasn't enough, was it?'

'Yes. Yes, it was.' Rachel took a steadying breath. 'But that wasn't the end of it.'

'What do you mean?'

'I mean...' Rachel knew there was no easy way to explain her reasons for seeing her aunt. 'Oh, Matt, I don't know why I did it, but—I went to see Aunt Maggie the afternoon you left for Geneva.'

'So?'

Matthew was unperturbed, and if Rachel had needed any further proof that he was innocent of any deception his attitude would have convinced her. But that didn't make her own task any easier.

'I had to see her,' she said at last. 'I know you may think it was foolish, but I wanted to confront her with her own lies. For so many years, I had believed everything she told me——' She broke off as the irony of that truth gripped her yet again. 'I was sure that this time I had the upper hand, and I wanted to tell her that, in spite of everything, we were going to get back together.'

'And?'

Matthew's eyes were almost sober now, and Rachel wondered how she could ever have disbelieved him.

'Well,' she said jerkily, 'it didn't work out the way I expected.'

'No?'

'No.' Rachel groaned. 'Oh, Matt, she said—she said Barbara had had a miscarriage——'

'She did.'

'I know that now. But Aunt Maggie said it was the baby she had been carrying when I left Penrith.'

Matthew blinked. 'But I told you, I hadn't touched Barbara before you left for London.'

'I know. I know.' Rachel could feel the hot tears pricking at the backs of her eyes. 'But—don't you see? She said you were the one who had been lying, not her. And—and——'

'You believed her.' Matthew's voice was harsh.

Rachel bent her head. 'Yes.'

'Why?'

'Oh, God, I don't know.' Rachel sniffed. 'I suppose I still couldn't believe she had been lying all these years.'

'But you believed I could?'

'No. Yes. Oh, I don't know. I've told you. I didn't know who to believe.'

'Even after I had told you about the pills!'

'I know.' Rachel felt terrible. 'I have no excuse for what I did, and actually your mother pointed out that if they were Barbara's pills then she couldn't possibly have got pregnant, even if——'

'Even if I had made love to her?' Matthew finished coldly. 'My God, you have some opinion of me, don't you? Even now.'

'No. *No!*' Rachel covered her face with her hands. 'You don't understand. So much had happened in so short a time, and I couldn't take it in——'

'You couldn't believe me.' Matthew sounded furious now. 'Hell, and you think that by coming here now you can ignore the past?'

Rachel's hands dropped to her throat. 'I—did think that,' she admitted huskily, clutching the frogged fastening of the cape. 'But—perhaps I was wrong——'

'You were!' he snarled, stepping closer to her, so that she could see the raw fury in his face. 'You bloody were,' he added. 'What do you think I am? Some kind of emotional tap, that can be turned on and off at will? Well, it's too late. Much too late. I don't need you, Rachel. I don't need anyone.'

Rachel couldn't take any more. A sob catching in her throat, she brushed past him and almost ran towards the door. She had to get away, she thought despairingly, before she humiliated herself utterly by bursting into tears in front of him. This was not one of the scenarios she had envisaged, and, no matter what Lady Olivia expected of her, she had to get out of there.

His hand embedded in the swirling mass of her hair arrested her, and she almost screamed at the pain he inflicted. 'Wait,' he muttered savagely, pressing his other hand flat against the door, preventing her from opening it, even had she had the strength to do so. 'Wait,' he said again, and now she felt his breath hot against the back of her neck. 'Damn you, Rachel, don't you walk out on me again.'

As his hand in her hair eased its pressure, Rachel turned so that her back was against the door and looked up at him through tear-filled eyes. 'I thought that was what you wanted,' she protested, and he uttered a defeated groan.

'Well, it's not,' he said thickly, his tone a mixture of hunger and frustration. 'I was always a fool where you were concerned. God, Rachel, why did you come here? Was it just because my mother asked you to, or did you really want to see me?'

'I really wanted to see you,' she assured him huskily, as his fingers disentangled themselves from the silky strands that were as reluctant to release him as she was. 'If I'd only never gone to see Aunt Maggie, none of this would have happened. I should have waited. I should have waited until you came back, and we could have gone to see her together.'

Matthew rested his forehead against hers. 'And now?'

She took a trembling breath. 'That's up to you.'

'Is it?' His fingers slid down her neck to the scented hollow of her throat. 'Is it really?' His thumbs probed the sensitive contours of her ears. 'And if I believe you, will you promise not to run out on me again without at least listening to my side of the story?'

'Yes. Oh, yes.' Rachel put up her hands to cover his, shaking her head against the hot tears that refused to be denied.

'Oh, love...'

His voice was hoarse as he lowered his mouth to hers, and she quivered uncontrollably as his warm lips rubbed gently against her yielding flesh. It was so long since he had kissed her, and the memories came flooding back. But, with infinite tenderness, Matthew licked away the treacherous tears that overspilled her eyes, and when his mouth returned to hers again there was a definite urgency to his kiss.

Keeping his mouth on hers, his hands found the lapels of her cape, parting the cloth so that when he rested his body against hers she was able to feel the heat of his lean frame.

'God, I can't believe this,' he muttered, cupping her face in his hands and gazing down at her with eyes that were both dark and pain-filled. 'Are you sure you know what you're doing? I won't let you go away again, you know. If you—if you stay here now, it's for good!'

The persistent rap at the door behind them was unnerving, but belatedly Rachel remembered she had ordered coffee for both of them.

'Um—Mrs Moffat,' she breathed, reluctantly trying to push him away from her, and with a supreme effort Matthew used the door on either side of her head to gain his balance.

'As you say,' he said, with the precise enunciation of someone who is not quite in control of himself, and as he moved away Rachel turned to open the door.

Mrs Moffat took in the scene she had interrupted with shrewd eyes, but if she was surprised to see Rachel she kept that particular observation to herself.

'This room smells like a brewery,' she declared bravely, bustling in to put the tray of coffee on the table, before opening a window to allow the cold night air into the library. 'And you must be tired, Miss Rachel,' she added, turning to her with a tight smile. 'I suggest you go and freshen up, and I'll have a nice little supper waiting for both of you when you come down.'

'That won't be necessary——' began Matthew, but Rachel overrode his denial.

'That would be lovely, Mrs Moffat,' she averred, avoiding her ex-husband's impatient gaze. 'I'm sure Matt could do with freshening up, too.'

'I'm sure he could,' agreed Mrs Moffat, taking advantage of Rachel's presence to voice thoughts she would otherwise never have dreamed of articulating. She looked at her employer with wary eyes. 'Is—er—is that all right, Mr Matt?'

'Why ask me?' enquired Matthew tersely, pouring himself a cup of black coffee and raising it grimly to his lips. 'Mrs—*Miss* Rachel appears to be giving the orders around here.'

Rachel sighed. 'Matt——'

'No. You go ahead,' he declared harshly, putting his empty cup back on the tray. 'As you both seem to think I'm in need of some immediate restoration, I'd better go and do something about it.'

'Matt——'

But he was already walking out of the room, albeit a little unsteadily, and, meeting Mrs Moffat's eyes, Rachel decided to let him go. They had plenty of time...

'Are you staying, Miss Rachel?'

Mrs Moffat's question brought her eyes back to the elderly housekeeper, and, putting her own thoughts aside for the moment, Rachel inclined her head. 'I hope so.'

'Well—thank goodness for that.' Mrs Moffat was relieved. 'Now perhaps things can go back to normal around here.'

Rachel smiled. 'Thank you.'

'Don't thank me. Just don't—change your mind again, will you?' exclaimed the housekeeper fervently. 'I don't think Mr Matt could stand it.'

After Mrs Moffat had gone to prepare the supper she had suggested, Rachel forced herself to drink a cup of coffee before going out to her car to rescue the suitcase she had left there earlier. Then she climbed the stairs to the first landing, turning instinctively towards the room she had occupied just four months ago. She had left here feeling so betrayed, she remembered, shivering. She must never let that happen again.

Evidently, Mrs Moffat had sent up one of the maids to turn down the bed, and lamplight glowed on creamy silk pillowcases and a pale lemon quilted duvet. Obviously, the housekeeper had not been prepared to speculate as to where Rachel might be spending the night, and the room was warm and welcoming.

Setting her suitcase on the ottoman at the foot of the bed, Rachel took off her cape and laid it over the arm of a chair. Outside, an owl swooped over the house, and she heard distinctly its eerie call as she peeled off the velvet jacket of her suit, and the olive-coloured blouse beneath. The skirt slid easily over her hips. Matthew was not the only one who had lost weight, she reflected, and, catching a glimpse of her reflection in the mirrors of the dressing-table, she wondered if he had noticed.

And where was he? she wondered, extracting a deep red dressing-gown from her case, and wrapping its silken folds about her. She had thought he might have been here, waiting for her, but evidently he had gone to his own suite of rooms.

She hesitated only a moment before opening her door again, and making her way along the corridor to where Matthew's apartments were situated. In spite of all that had gone before, she was still nervous, and it took every ounce of courage she had to open the door to his sitting-room and step inside.

Closing the door again, she leaned back against it, and as she did so she heard the sound of running water. Obviously he was taking a shower, and, although her instincts urged her to go through the bedroom and into the bathroom, there were some things she just could not do. It had been ten years, after all, she reminded herself unsteadily. And just because she was swamped with painful memories, there was no reason to suppose Matthew felt the same.

All the same, she could not remain glued to the bedroom door, and, taking a deep breath, she stepped away from the supporting panels. Matthew's rooms, *the rooms they had once shared*, had changed, too. Whereas, when they had lived together, there had been some feminine influence in their design, now they were almost starkly masculine, and she wondered why Barbara had never imprinted her personality upon them.

But thinking about Barbara was still too painful to bear, and instead she moved on, through the plain gold and brown austerity of his sitting-room, to his bedroom door.

Like the sitting-room, the bedroom was decorated in shades of beige and brown, the only splash of colour the multicoloured pattern of the quilt that covered the enormous king-sized bed. It was the bed they had chosen together when they'd first got married, and thinking of him sharing *that* with Barbara was almost unbearable.

She was standing there, staring at the bed, when Matthew appeared in the bathroom doorway. Evidently he had not heard her come into his apartments, and his eyes met hers with obvious wariness, before the awareness of his own lack of covering caused him to step back.

'Don't—don't go!' exclaimed Rachel hastily, her eyes shifting from his face, and the light covering of dark hair on his chest, to the flat planes of his stomach, where more hair arrowed down to his sex. It was the first time she had seen Matthew naked for so long, and although he was painfully thin he was still the most beautiful man she had ever seen. 'Oh, Matt,' she breathed, as his body shifted revealingly beneath her eyes. 'I love you. I love you so much.'

She covered the space between them in milliseconds, and when his arm closed around her, imprisoning her against his hard body, she knew a marvellous feeling of homecoming. Winding her arms about his waist, she pressed herself against him, and his hardening body fitted naturally against the yielding softness of hers.

'I want you,' he groaned, his tongue sliding between her lips to ravage the trembling contours of her mouth. 'God—you don't know how much!'

'I have some idea,' she breathed huskily, slipping her hand between them and touching his throbbing hardness. 'Oh, Matt, make love to me, *please*! I need you. I need you so much.'

The quilt that covered the bed was soft and cool against her bare back as Matthew knelt over her. The red silk dressing-gown had been discarded on to the warm beige carpet, and Matthew was gaining a certain amount of satisfaction from divesting her of the remaining items of her clothing. She had not been wearing a bra, but she was still wearing lacy bikini briefs, and gossamer-fine black tights, and, although Matthew was as eager as she was to consummate their loveplay, as he peeled her tights off her legs he followed them with his lips.

'Soft—so soft,' he breathed unsteadily, finding the sensitive skin of her inner thigh and probing the soft curls at the junction of her legs. 'Dear lord, Rachel, this is not going to be a prolonged seduction, I'm afraid. I need you now. This minute! Oh, God, you're so beautiful! How have I ever lived without this——?'

Rachel flinched a little as he slid into her. It had been so long. But it was a marvellous feeling, knowing his body was joined to hers once again, and she wound her arms around his neck to bring him closer, arching her hips up to his.

It was over almost too soon, although the pulsating heat that shook her body long after Matthew had collapsed on top of her kept her on a high of ecstasy for many mindless minutes. She hadn't forgotten Matthew, but she had forgotten the perfection of their love-making, and when he would have drawn away she wrapped her legs around him, and kept him where he was.

'Do you have any idea what you're doing to me?' he groaned, burying his face between her breasts, and as he swelled inside her she uttered a contented giggle.

'I have a pretty good idea,' she breathed, and as he levered himself up on his elbows to look down at her she laved one of his hard nipples with her tongue.

'You said we had to talk,' he reminded her thickly, finding the parted sweetness of her mouth, but Rachel didn't want to talk right then.

'Later,' she whispered, her nails digging possessively into his narrow buttocks. 'Mmm, Matt, do that again! I love it...'

Evidently, Mrs Moffat had decided against reminding them that she was preparing supper. A couple of hours later, Rachel opened her eyes to find Matthew propped up on one elbow looking down at her, and it was obvious the thought of food was the last thing on his mind, too.

'You're the only woman I know who looks just as good asleep as awake,' he murmured, lowering his head to caress her lips with his tongue, and although Rachel didn't much care for the comparison she decided to be charitable.

'You've had a lot of experience, I suppose,' she ventured, trying to make light of it, but her pain was not as easy to hide as she had thought.

'Not a lot, no,' Matthew replied gently, understanding her feelings. 'And since you came back into my life, there's been no one else.'

Rachel moistened her dry lips. 'Was there—before?'

'When Barbara was alive, you mean?' Matthew's lips twisted. 'Some, I guess. As I told you before, Barbara and I did not have a real marriage.'

'Not—not ever?'

'Oh...' Matthew groaned and rolled on to his back, raising his arm to shade his eyes against the warm glow from the lamp on the table beside the bed. 'Well, we had a sexual relationship for a while. But it didn't work out. That's the simple answer, at least.'

'And the unsimple one?'

'God!' Matthew ran weary fingers through the tumbled thickness of his hair. 'We had so many problems. Once my initial desire to hurt you was blunted, it was easy to see the holes in our relationship. We had nothing in common, for a start. Barbara liked travelling, spending money on expensive clothes and jewels, going to parties! I didn't. And she hated being pregnant.

I'm pretty sure that was why she lost the first baby. But she knew that two miscarriages would look pretty suspicious, and I suppose she was prepared to do anything to secure her position. But, once she was pregnant again, things went from bad to worse. We used to row all the time, and she told me she had only married me because—well, because she was jealous of you.'

'She hated me, you mean.' Rachel shivered. 'Oh, Matt.'

She turned her face into his chest, and pressed her lips against the hair-roughened skin. His skin smelt warm and musky, and when she touched him with her tongue he tasted sharply masculine.

He shuddered under her caressing lips, but he had to go on. 'After Rosemary was born, she hardly saw her mother. Barbara was never there. I suspected there were other men, but I didn't care. I had no desire to start divorce proceedings, and maybe run the risk of Barbara's getting custody of Rosemary. But even that wasn't enough.'

'What do you mean?'

Matthew heaved a sigh. 'I don't know why she did it now. Maybe she already knew she was ill, and it was her way of taking her revenge. In any event, she evidently resented the love I had for our daughter, because when Rosemary was six years old she told me that I wasn't the child's father.'

'No!' Rachel blinked and sat up. 'Why would she do that?'

'Perhaps it was the truth.'

'No!' Rachel was adamant. 'She was lying.'

'Was she?'

'Of course she was.' Rachel shifted, and Matthew's eyes darkened as the lamplight glinted on her small breasts, swollen and erect from his lovemaking. 'Rosemary's your daughter. How could you doubt it?'

'Well——' Matthew expelled a breath '—lately, I have come to the conclusion that you might be right. But for months—years, even—I couldn't be certain.'

'Oh, Matt!'

'Well, you have to admit, *we* were married for almost four years, and we never had any children——'

'You know why.' Rachel stared at him helplessly. 'Besides——'

'In any case, Barbara accused me of being incapable of siring a child, and you don't know what that does to a man.'

'Oh, God!'

Rachel was horrified, but now she could understand so much. Not least, why Matthew and his daughter had been so estranged.

'I guess it was her way of hurting me. And I tried not to let it affect my feelings for Rosemary, but it did,' he muttered heavily. 'Until—until you came back——'

'Me?'

'Yes, you.' Matthew closed his eyes for a moment. 'I think it was seeing you two together; realising what I had lost. I know I was jealous, at first. Jealous of you, and jealous of Rosemary. It was only when you had that fall, and I thought I'd killed you, that I realised what was wrong. I realised, too, that it didn't really matter whether Rosemary was my child or not. She thought she was, and that was all that mattered.'

Rachel shook her head, leaning over him so that the pointed tips of her breasts were brushing his chest. 'She *is* your daughter,' she told him huskily. 'Anyone can see that.' She caught her breath. 'Why else do you think she's so provoking?'

Matthew's hand behind her head brought her mouth to his. 'So long as I provoke you,' he said unsteadily.

'Oh, you do,' she breathed, smoothing her thumbs across his cheeks. Then she shook her head again. 'Poor Barbara! You know, I can almost feel sorry for her now.'

'You're very charitable.'

'Yes—well, I'm very lucky,' said Rachel shakily. 'After all, I've got both of you, haven't I? You and Rosemary.'

Matthew bit his lip. 'And if we don't have any more children, you won't mind?'

'But we *will*!' Rachel sighed, and then she added softly, 'I wasn't going to tell you this. Not yet, at any rate. But—I had a miscarriage, too. Just—just a few days after I arrived in London.'

Matthew stared at her then, his eyes wide and comprehending. 'Our child!' he muttered disbelievingly. 'Oh, God! Our child!'

'Our son, actually,' she admitted, the memory of that awful occasion still having the power to bring the tears to her eyes. Determinedly, she blinked them away. 'But we'll have others. If—if it's what you want.'

'If it's what I want?' he groaned, rolling over so that she was imprisoned beneath him. 'God, you know what I want. But is it what you want? Downstairs—downstairs, I told you it was all—or nothing, and I thought you looked pretty relieved when Mrs Moffat interrupted us.'

'Did you?' Rachel's lips twisted now. 'Oh, darling, if I looked relieved when Mrs Moffat interrupted us it was probably because I was in danger of tearing your clothes off there and then, and somehow I don't think your housekeeper would have approved.'

Matthew buried his face in her neck. 'And— Harcourt?' he muttered, as if he was dreading her answer and didn't want to see her face when she made it.

'He's found a replacement,' whispered Rachel gently. 'A young man called Alan Maxwell. I can assure you, he's much more to Justin's taste than I ever was.'

Matthew lifted his head to look at her. 'Are you serious?'

'Do I look serious?' she asked, touching his mouth with her fingers, and he caressed each one with his lips.

'You look—beautiful,' he told her huskily. 'The most beautiful woman I have ever known.' He paused. 'You won't mind living here again, will you? I mean——' He broke off. 'I know it must have unhappy associations.'

Rachel shook her head. 'Not now. Not now that we're together again.' She took a breath. 'Did—did you redecorate these rooms after Barbara died?'

'Barbara never shared these rooms,' said Matthew roughly. 'That was one betrayal I couldn't make. We—slept in one of the other bedrooms. While we were sleeping together, that is. Long before she told me about Rosemary, I had moved back in here.'

Rachel couldn't deny the overwhelming feeling of relief she knew right then. She pitied Barbara, and she was sorry she was dead. But she was glad that Matthew had kept their love inviolate.

'About Rosemary,' she ventured now, 'do you think she will mind if—if I come to live here?'

'If you marry me, you mean,' Matthew corrected her softly. 'Let's have no more misunderstandings. I love you, and I want you to be my wife. And you know Rosemary will be delighted. She's very fond of you.'

'Honestly?'

'Honestly,' he assured her. 'And from now on that's going to be the only thing between us. Agreed?'

'Agreed,' she conceded, somewhat unsteadily. And there didn't seem a lot more to say...

PASSPORT TO ROMANCE VACATION SWEEPSTAKES

OFFICIAL RULES

SWEEPSTAKES RULES AND REGULATIONS. NO PURCHASE NECESSARY.
HOW TO ENTER:

1. To enter, complete this official entry form and return with your invoice in the envelope provided, or print your name, address, telephone number and age on a plain piece of paper and mail to: Passport to Romance, P.O. Box #1397, Buffalo, N.Y. 14269-1397. No mechanically reproduced entries accepted.

2. All entries must be received by the Contest Closing Date, midnight, December 31, 1990 to be eligible.

3. Prizes: There will be ten (10) Grand Prizes awarded, each consisting of a choice of a trip for two people to: i) London, England (approximate retail value $5,050 U.S.); ii) England, Wales and Scotland (approximate retail value $6,400 U.S.); iii) Caribbean Cruise (approximate retail value $7,300 U.S.); iv) Hawaii (approximate retail value $9,550 U.S.); v) Greek Island Cruise in the Mediterranean (approximate retail value $12,250 U.S.); vi) France (approximate retail value $7,300 U.S.).

4. Any winner may choose to receive any trip or a cash alternative prize of $5,000.00 U.S. in lieu of the trip.

5. Odds of winning depend on number of entries received.

6. A random draw will be made by Nielsen Promotion Services, an independent judging organization on January 29, 1991, in Buffalo, N.Y., at 11:30 a.m. from all eligible entries received on or before the Contest Closing Date. Any Canadian entrants who are selected must correctly answer a time-limited, mathematical skill-testing question in order to win. Quebec residents may submit any litigation respecting the conduct and awarding of a prize in this contest to the Régie des loteries et courses du Quebec.

7. Full contest rules may be obtained by sending a stamped, self-addressed envelope to: "Passport to Romance Rules Request", P.O. Box 9998, Saint John, New Brunswick, E2L 4N4.

8. Payment of taxes other than air and hotel taxes is the sole responsibility of the winner.

9. Void where prohibited by law.

PASSPORT TO ROMANCE VACATION SWEEPSTAKES

OFFICIAL RULES

SWEEPSTAKES RULES AND REGULATIONS. NO PURCHASE NECESSARY.
HOW TO ENTER:

1. To enter, complete this official entry form and return with your invoice in the envelope provided, or print your name, address, telephone number and age on a plain piece of paper and mail to: Passport to Romance, P.O. Box #1397, Buffalo, N.Y. 14269-1397. No mechanically reproduced entries accepted.

2. All entries must be received by the Contest Closing Date, midnight, December 31, 1990 to be eligible.

3. Prizes: There will be ten (10) Grand Prizes awarded, each consisting of a choice of a trip for two people to: i) London, England (approximate retail value $5,050 U.S.); ii) England, Wales and Scotland (approximate retail value $6,400 U.S.); iii) Caribbean Cruise (approximate retail value $7,300 U.S.); iv) Hawaii (approximate retail value $9,550 U.S.); v) Greek Island Cruise in the Mediterranean (approximate retail value $12,250 U.S.); vi) France (approximate retail value $7,300 U.S.).

4. Any winner may choose to receive any trip or a cash alternative prize of $5,000.00 U.S. in lieu of the trip.

5. Odds of winning depend on number of entries received.

6. A random draw will be made by Nielsen Promotion Services, an independent judging organization on January 29, 1991, in Buffalo, N.Y., at 11:30 a.m. from all eligible entries received on or before the Contest Closing Date. Any Canadian entrants who are selected must correctly answer a time-limited, mathematical skill-testing question in order to win. Quebec residents may submit any litigation respecting the conduct and awarding of a prize in this contest to the Régie des loteries et courses du Quebec.

7. Full contest rules may be obtained by sending a stamped, self-addressed envelope to: "Passport to Romance Rules Request", P.O. Box 9998, Saint John, New Brunswick, E2L 4N4.

8. Payment of taxes other than air and hotel taxes is the sole responsibility of the winner

9. Void where prohibited by law.

PASSPORT
WIN
1 of 10 Vacations
SEE INSIDE
TO ROMANCE

VACATION SWEEPSTAKES
Official Entry Form

MONTH 3 ENTRY

Yes, enter me in the drawing for one of ten Vacations-for-Two! If I'm a winner, I'll get my choice of any of the six different destinations being offered — and I won't have to decide until after I'm notified!

Return entries with invoice in envelope provided along with Daily Travel Allowance Voucher. Each book in your shipment has two entry forms — and the more you enter, the better your chance of winning!

Name _____

Address _____ Apt. _____

City _____ State/Prov. _____ Zip/Postal Code _____

Daytime phone number _____
                         Area Code

☐ I am enclosing a Daily Travel Allowance Voucher in the amount of $ _____ Write in amount revealed beneath scratch-off

© 1990 HARLEQUIN ENTERPRISES LTD.

PASSPORT
WIN
1 of 10 Vacations
SEE INSIDE
TO ROMANCE

VACATION SWEEPSTAKES
Official Entry Form

MONTH 3 ENTRY

Yes, enter me in the drawing for one of ten Vacations-for-Two! If I'm a winner, I'll get my choice of any of the six different destinations being offered — and I won't have to decide until after I'm notified!

Return entries with invoice in envelope provided along with Daily Travel Allowance Voucher. Each book in your shipment has two entry forms — and the more you enter, the better your chance of winning!

Name _____

Address _____ Apt. _____

City _____ State/Prov. _____ Zip/Postal Code _____

Daytime phone number _____
                         Area Code

☐ I am enclosing a Daily Travel Allowance Voucher in the amount of $ _____ Write in amount revealed beneath scratch-off

CPS-THREE